Daniel Leydon

Uncle Bob,
Thanks for being a

SOMEONE,
SOMEWHERE

great friend to me
and my family.

A D&D
Investigations
Caper

outskirtspress
DENVER, COLORADO

Someone, Somewhere
A D&D Investigations Caper

Outskirts Press, Inc.
http://www.outskirtspress.com

Paperback ISBN: 978-1-4787-4597-6
Hardback ISBN: 978-1-4787-4683-6

Outskirts Press and the "OP" logo are trademarks belonging to Outskirts Press, Inc.

PRINTED IN THE UNITED STATES OF AMERICA

Chapter One

*I*guess the entire school district is going through an epidemic! Denise Lawson thought to herself. Out of habit, she broke the word down in her head. Because while Denise liked a lot of things, she *loved* words! She was Santa Maria Academy's representative in the National Spelling Bee just last month, so she was still in the habit of spelling words that intrigued her. E-p-i-d-e-m-i-c was one.

The flu season was off to a roaring start in El Paso, and the whole city was buzzing. In fact the KPEP News Team had even done a story on it last night. Sure, January was a slow news month, but still this was getting a lot of attention!

A "health crisis" was how Mrs. Caramia, her fourth grade teacher, described this plague. And, according to the Health Department, the School Department, and every other department around, there was only one thing that could stop this overwhelming march of attacking microbes, which appeared to have nothing better to do than pick on the poor, well-meaning kids of Santa Maria.

What could this miracle cure be? Surely, some geeky scientist squirreled away in a dark and dreary underground laboratory had happened upon an ultra-complex formula of chemicals, herbs, and insect body parts that magically transformed into...ta-da! The divine answer that would forever keep kids from missing uncountable days of precious school!

Aaahhh—no! The miracle the teachers were talking about was...wait for it... HAND SANITIZER!

"Wow!" Denise whispered to her seatmate and best friend, Mimi DelaVega. "Why didn't I think of that? It's pure genius! Wash your hands and never have to worry about runny noses and throwing up again!"

While dabbing her favorite vanilla lip gloss on her lips, Denise suddenly realized that Mrs. Caramia appeared alarmed. The teacher announced, "We used up all our hand sanitizers! We need a couple of volunteers to go get some more boxes so we can, hopefully, prevent the rest of you from getting sick."

Denise allowed herself a little daydream and imagined for a minute staying home for a few days. *Wait,* she thought, *it might not be too bad to catch a few* Phineas and Ferb *marathons, eat some S'mores Goldfish, rearrange my extensive hair bow collection, and especially, read to my heart's content.* There was nothing Denise liked more than sitting, lying, or even standing, and reading chapter after chapter of a good book.

Denise suddenly remembered what happened in third grade when her brother Jacob (a.k.a. her mortal enemy) and she had been stricken by the flu of *last* season. She did stay home for three days, but the misery of throwing up—boy, did she hate throwing up—getting chills and then a fever brought her back to reality. She even had to miss her gymnastics class, which she *loved.* Yeah, that experience was actually in the negative column!

She had noticed that about half the seats in the classroom were empty. Likewise the cafeteria and schoolyard didn't seem the same without so many of her friends.

"Anyone? Anyone? Two people right after lunch," repeated Mrs. Caramia.

Denise really liked Mrs. Caramia. She had helped her so much to prepare for the spelling bee, and she always encouraged her when Denise secretly told her about problems she was having with some of the other kids in class. When it came right down to it, Denise actually liked school. To top it off, it was Friday and she felt like a little mini-adventure might be a great way to start the weekend early.

Denise and Mimi exchanged glances from their seats. The friends had developed a way of communicating without having to actually say anything.

"Well, yes, *we* will volunteer to bring back some hand sanitizer, Mrs. Caramia," said Denise as she and Mimi waved their hands in the air. "Just point us in the right direction and we will single-handedly or double-handedly save the school from this treacherous plague." In her head, Denise quickly spelled "*t-r-e-a-c-h-e-r-o-u-s.*"

"Thanks, kids. I knew I could count on you two! Come back here right after lunch."

Almost immediately the bell rang and everyone went to the cafeteria for lunch. No sooner had Denise put her tray at the seat beside Mimi when she felt as if someone was staring at her. She turned and who do you suppose was glaring at her with that evil eye? The one girl in the whole school who caused her drama. The one girl in the whole school who could ruin her day, make her stomach feel like it was full of hot coals. The one girl who could paralyze her and make her speechless with a mere look or comment. The girl she called her "arch-nemesis," Amanda Lucas. Mandy!

"Why are they sending a kid with breath like rotten eggs to get a job done? The only thing lamer than those four-eyes pair of glasses on you are those wretched shoes! Have you been shopping at the Goodwill store again?" the mean girl sneered.

Denise froze. She felt her cheeks blazing and her throat closing. Her mind raced, trying to think of something to say, but she was too overwhelmed. It was always like this. She would think of some witty and cutting response tonight when she was home. But for now she hung her head and looked straight ahead. Embarrassed, humiliated—she felt like everyone in the cafeteria had heard Mandy's nasty insults and were staring at her. In her mind, the whole school knew she was being insulted. She felt so small!

As Mandy walked away, Mimi kicked her friend under the table. "Geez, Denise, I can't believe you don't say something back to that little twerp. Everyone knows she's just jealous of you! But you have to put her in her place...she's not half as smart or pretty as you...you should know that!"

"I don't know what happens, Mimi... I feel so helpless when she says things. It makes me so embarrassed and I know I should say something, but I just freeze up! She makes me feel awful!"

The friends ate in silence for a little while. Mimi had seen that pained look on Denise before. She decided to tell Denise a funny story about being in a Christmas play and her angel costume getting torn off because it got caught on a nail.

Denise began to chuckle. It was true, for some reason, nothing seemed to go smoothly for Mimi. But she somehow kept a positive attitude. She smiled to herself. "I know what you're trying to do, you know, Meems."

Mimi opened her eyes and mouth wide in mock shock. "Me? Whatever do you mean?" she cried.

They both threw back their heads and laughed hard. Denise loved to laugh, and she could feel the tension and shame melting away. Things were back to normal. They turned their thoughts to their "assignment."

"Well, this should be a cool break for us, actually. Friday afternoons are always so boring," Denise said cheerily, now running a lemony lip gloss over her pursed lips. In case it wasn't obvious, Denise was a lip gloss fanatic.

"I just hope it's not too much work," Mimi said, giving Denise a quiet little smile. "C'mon. Let's get this done."

They walked over to their classroom and were met by their teacher.

"Hey, you guys," exclaimed Mrs. Caramia. "Here's what you do… At the beginning of the year, we stockpiled all the supplies for the elementary school kids and had them tucked away in a storage space that we're using this year. Go see Mrs. England and she'll give you the keys and instructions."

With the word "keys," Denise felt odd; warm waves pass through her body. She had felt those waves before and had learned that they didn't mean anything good. Something was not quite right, she knew. She also knew that time would soon tell her exactly what it was about this situation that had her on alert. Her father called these feelings "instincts" and was always telling her to trust them and to keep trying to recognize them when they popped up.

Her father was always giving her these kinds of tips. Well…it was only natural since he spent over thirty years as a cop, so it just stayed in his blood. He retired from the San Francisco Police Department, and the family all moved to El Paso. Of course, he couldn't just stop "fighting crime," as he called it, so he and Denise formed what he believed to be the best father-daughter detective agency in the world—D &D Investigations. They always get their man. Of course things were a little slow right now being that they just got started. But they were expecting great things. Denise loved the idea of being able to figure things out on her own. It made her feel way more grown up.

Whether this feeling was instinct, fear, or indigestion, she would have to go through with her "mission." After all, she and her BFF were on the case, and they had always proven to be a formidable team.

Mrs. England's office was close by, and the girls were there before they even had time to discuss what was going on. Denise definitely didn't have time to mention her feeling to Mimi. *Just as well*, she thought as Mrs. England welcomed them in and shut the door. Denise caught a glimpse of her reflection in the glass door to the huge bookcase behind Mrs. England's cluttered desk. The most prominent feature on the girl looking back at her was the large blue and white polka-dotted hair bow that was pinned to the back of her light brown hair. Denise loved hair bows, and this one was a gift from her grandfather, who was the master of gift-giving and spoiling. He called himself "The Genius-at-Large," for he was able to build, fix, or do just about anything. The hair bow made it look a little bit like she had cat ears, and the glasses completed what could best be described as a "studious" look. With her ponytail down past her shoulders and pretty heart-shaped face, she was quite pleased with the look as a whole. All the Santa Maria girls had to wear the same white polos and red plaid jumpers, so Denise liked to add some personal touches to make herself feel unique.

"...going to need at least four boxes..."

Denise suddenly realized that Mrs. England had been talking the whole time she was analyzing her studious look. She furrowed her brow in a fairly weak attempt at pretending to concentrate. Mrs. England was a serious but pleasant woman with round glasses and short gray hair. She looked exactly like, well, a school principal... Funny how that works.

"...so you'll have to get the cart from the cafeteria and bring it up to the old high school building. You know, we haven't used it for years, since the new building went up. We have a storage room way up on the sixth floor where the janitors put our supply stock. These are the keys." She held up a large chain with a ring that held about ten keys. Denise had seen a key chain like this before because her mother, Stella Lawson, actually worked in a prison—not many kids could say that—and this is how they carried keys...on big chains.

"This big one opens the outside front door; the elevator is just inside on the right-hand side...it's a little old but it passes inspection every six months. Get out on the sixth floor and room number 606 is down the hall on the right. This key with 606 taped to it fits the door, and the sanitizer should be right there. Okay, girls. Thanks for doing this. We need to get a handle on these flu bugs!"

Denise and Mimi listened while staring at Mrs. England wordlessly. About halfway through Denise wondered, *Is Mimi thinking what I'm thinking...Keys? Carts? Elevator? ARE YOU SERIOUS? I thought this was an easy job—go to a closet somewhere near the bathroom...the cafeteria at the furthest, carry a few boxes. Come back heroes. Are you serious?*

Tiny Santa Maria Academy was an El Paso treasure, best known for preparing young kids for college, and they had a wonderful track record. For one hundred years young ladies from the Texas and Mexico area had been sent off to the finest colleges and universities in the world. To say that the bar was set high was an understatement. In their few years at the school, Denise and Mimi had learned to expect to be challenged.

The campus sat about halfway up one of the lower mountain slopes that dominated El Paso's rough terrain. The Spanish-style buildings were old but well-kept. First-time visitors were always drawn to the beautiful chapel with its bell tower. The low lands, the Rio Grande River, and then Mexico spread majestically below as you made your way along the grounds.

Dutifully Denise took the keys and walked out of the office with Mimi. As they trudged—and, yes, they were trudging—outside and started toward the cafeteria building, they stared up at the large hulking building at the top of the hill. During the last few years they had run up and down the pathways that wound between many of the buildings on the Santa Maria campus without giving much thought to anything but the classrooms, the cafeteria, and the chapel. They were aware of the Administration Building, the gym, and the high school, but the "old high school" was the one place on campus that seemed to have a personality of its own. A squat cube of yellow and brown adobe brick that sat like a sphinx on top of its perch. It overlooked every nook and cranny with eyes thinly disguised as windows. Staring at the ribbon of a path leading to its door like a tongue to a waiting mouth.

This foreboding appearance was only one of the idea bubbles bouncing around inside of Denise's suddenly overwhelmed brain. Each girl was now wondering if the other had heard the whispered rumors or felt the uneasy chills that shivered through them on the few occasions that they had even dared to go near the ominous structure.

Mimi was a third-generation Santa Maria student and a native of El Paso. She had heard the stories about the scary old building for as long as she could remember. She had shared a few with Denise, but to be honest, she had suppressed most of them because she never thought in a million years that she would have to go anywhere near it, let alone go inside this monster posing as a building.

Still, she had to tell Denise...

"Hey, Denise," Mimi began, timidly. "Do you believe in ghosts?"

Chapter Two

Denise could not believe her ears as she singsonged, "Aaaaaahhhhh, yea-uh I do-oo. I believe you know that, being my best friend and everything. Do you?"

"Well, I probably wouldn't—except my mother, sister, grandmother, grandfather, and neighbors have told me the same stories since I can remember, and almost all of them had something to do with the building that we're about to go into!"

"What?...What?...What? Why didn't you say something!?"

"Well, we're always talking about being brave enough and smart enough to do anything, so I didn't want Mrs. England to think that we couldn't handle a simple assignment."

"What in the world is this ghost thing...? And how in the world can it be in the one place on earth that we have to go to get hand sanitizer so the Academy doesn't get decimated by the flu? Am I being too dramatic?"

"Actually, you've summed it up perfectly. There is an ancient Mexican legend of a creature called La Lucheza, or the Owl Lady—half witch, half bird. This one lives in the belfry of that building. She tries to lure children close by imitating crying babies or animals. Then she snatches them up in her claws and flies away with them…never to be seen again!"

"Oh, gee, that's a *great* ghost story," sputtered Denise. "So we're gonna get snatched up by a giant owl lady witch and get carried away to God-knows-where if we go near that building?!" The two friends looked down for a few seconds to try and think.

"Come on, Mimi, those things only happen at night…if ever. People tell these stories just to scare each other. Let's do this—we walk up real fast, we open the door, we take the elevator up, we find room 606, we get the boxes, we come back, and we're done! We move so fast we don't even have

time to think about anything that can go wrong or scare us!"
Denise talked so fast she was out of breath by the time she
finished. That's what happens when you're trying to convince
yourself you're not terrified.

Denise and Mimi were walking extra-fast over to the cafeteria, which was next door to their classrooms, and noticed
that the Pre-K class of four-year-olds was having unstructured
playtime. The girls knew that these were simply code words
for "chaos." Denise, the spelling bee queen of Santa Maria,
even knew that the origin of the word "c-h-a-o-s" was Greek.
But that was not on the radar right now because she was
watching a scene that made her mad.

The biggest preschooler on campus, a four-foot, fifty-five-
pound brute, was gleefully terrorizing one of Denise's favorite
little girl students, Marisella, by holding her Pinkie Pie Pony
over her head, just out of reach. The little girl was wailing
steadily while she jumped over and over, only to have the bigger boy pull it out of reach.

"Hey, Brutus!" Denise yelled, for yes, difficult as that may be to believe, this was the little ruffian's name. "I'm gonna take a picture of you with Pinkie Pie so everyone's going to know that you like My Little Pony." She held up her wallet, which was pink and was going to have to suffice as a prop to bluff a four-year-old into believing that it was a phone camera.

"I hate My Little Pony! That's for girls!" bellowed Brutus the brute.

"That's not what we heard," Mimi replied, thus joining in the trick rescue of poor little Marisella. "We're watching you, Brutus. Leave the little ones alone."

"Aw, man...I was just playin'!"

Having effortlessly thwarted—another spelling word—a four-year-old's attempt at bullying, the two friends began to get down to the real business of saving the school from the dreaded influenza. On the way to the cafeteria, Mimi told Denise, "The only thing I hate worse than seeing a little kid in distress is seeing someone hurting an animal!"

Denise was very aware of Mimi's affection for anything that was warm and furry. She had two dogs and a puppy at home, and those were only the ones that Denise knew about. Denise? She liked animals but not enough to keep one as a pet; she preferred to spend her quiet time with her books. Give her some *Dork Diaries* any day!

Okay, first stop was the cafeteria to grab the cart. When they went inside they found Mrs. Croquette busily counting money at the cash register. "Hey, Mrs. C!" called Denise. "We need to borrow the hand cart to carry some supplies."

"Well, it's right over there," replied Mrs. C., pointing toward the corner closet. "But it's going to drive you crazy because of the wobbly wheel. No matter how many times the guy fixes it, it always goes back to being the squeaky, rumbly cart. I don't even use it anymore." The girls looked over and saw a run-of-the-mill metal cart about four feet long.

Denise went over and began pushing. Sure enough, three wheels were smooth as could be, but the front right wobbled and shook like the Lost Gold Mine ride at Peter Piper Pizza. The wheel screeched constantly and the wobble made it about three times harder to push than it should, besides driving them both crazy.

"This mission is really off on the wrong foot," Denise huffed to Mimi out the side of her mouth.

Seeing that the effort was getting Denise cranky, Mimi attempted a little cheering-up. "Let's keep a positive attitude. It'll be an adventure."

"Well, since you're in such an adventurous mood, what do you say you give me a hand pushing this monstrosity of a cart up that monstrosity of a hill!" cried Denise. She visualized the spelling of m-o-n-s-t-r-o-s-i-t-y.

As our heroes pushed the cart up the incline to the waiting monster, a steady, incredibly annoying soundtrack accompanied them on their grand adventure. DEEDLE-eet, DEEDLE-eet, DEEDLE-eeet!

"Good grief! If there really is an owl-lady-witch thing

living there, we just woke her and any other creature totally up!" Denise yelled over the racket.

"I don't know, Denise. Maybe it will scare anyone or any spirit away long enough for us to get in and get out. I think this is a good thing!"

"Mimi, that positive attitude is gonna take you a long way, someday," admitted Denise.

"Well, I hope it starts today," murmured Mimi.

Denise felt like she was watching a movie as she approached the dusty brown double doors. As she peered into the old building, she got the shivering feeling that it was looking right back at her. And since she also loved metaphors, it felt like a cat watching a canary.

Determined to show maturity and responsibility, despite being, basically, petrified, Denise forced herself to open the door with the big key. Surprisingly it fit fine and the door opened without any trouble, any creaking, or any creatures. There was only one thing to do. Keep moving forward.

As the girls stepped inside, they immediately noticed a yellow Day-Glo poster on the wall next to the elevators.

SENIOR CLASS OF 1978

INVITES YOU TO A GRAND PERFORMANCE

OF SLEEPING BEAUTY

FRIDAY AND SATURDAY NIGHTS 8 PM

"Nineteen seventy-eight?!" they exclaimed in stereo.

"You've got to be kidding me!! My mom was born in 1978!" Mimi squealed.

Denise could feel the damp air on her skin, and she could see what must have been a million pieces of dust illuminated in the dozen or so shafts of sunlight that cut diagonally through the lobby of the old school. Yeah, it was creepy—but she could see okay, so she kept moving... She had decided that this was going to be the key...don't stop and think. Only bad things can happen if you stop and think. Having Mimi beside her was a huge help in sticking to the strategy, because she probably wouldn't even have come this far alone.

Luckily the elevator was easy to operate, too. It had a big black light switch, which Mimi happily turned on, and big black round buttons with the floor numbers.

As Denise wrestled the cart onto the elevator, she inadvertently, but with great pleasure, discovered a trick to quiet the obnoxious wheel. "Hey, all you have to do is push down on the back and this thing actually doesn't work too bad at all."

"Now you tell me! Well, number six, here we come!" said Mimi. The button made a squishing noise as she pushed it, and they felt the elevator come to life.

"Let's get this over with," muttered Denise.

The old elevator still had some pent-up power from all the years of sitting idle, for when they arrived on the sixth floor, the car stopped suddenly with a little bounce just to let them know who was boss. For a second they had a feeling of weightlessness, which immediately mixed with their other creepy feelings, and the combination was not good. In fact, not good at all. "Oooohhh!" they both cried squeamishly. The doors noisily slid aside and they stepped out.

Down the hallway, to the right, just as Mrs. England had described were the even-numbered classrooms. Bigger shafts of light gave the girls plenty of light to see, but that wasn't the problem right now.

Both girls froze stock-still as a faint, otherworldly cry rose from deep inside the building somewhere and began to build. *Aaaaarrrrhhhh aaarrhhh-ah-ah arrHHH!*

"Oooohhh." They both sucked in their breath and didn't move a muscle.

"Do you see anything?" whispered Denise in the quietest voice she had ever used.

Mimi's eyes were open so wide that Denise could see every vein inside them.

"No. It sounded kind of like a puppy, though."

"A puppy or a baby," Denise answered.

Denise wondered if Mimi remembered the part of the legend where La Lucheza tried to lure kids close to their fate. Hmm.

"Actually, it could have been the elevator. I don't hear anything now. L-L-Let's go," Mimi declared bravely.

The classrooms all had window shades covering the large panes of glass on the top half of the doors. And wouldn't you know—the shades on room 600, 602, and 604 were all rolled up so you could see inside. Down the hall you could see that rooms 608 and 610 had their shades up, too.

Only in room 606—the one place that they had to go, the one place that they wanted to see inside—was the shade down. If they had listed all the things that were included in their plan, being able to see inside the room would be number one on the list! And the shade was completely down; they couldn't see a thing inside.

They sidled over to the front of the door nervously. Denise looked at Mimi, and Mimi looked at Denise. Denise's heart was pumping so hard she felt like she could hear it.

Using their BFF communication skills, Denise whispered firmly, "When I count to three, let's both pull the shade and we can see what's inside!" Mimi nodded meekly and placed her hand on the bottom of the shade. Denise did the same and said, "One—twooo—two and a haaalllfff—THREE!"

They both pulled down one inch and let go. SNAP! The shade flew up and hit the top with a slap. In a split second the girls saw the most grotesque, evil, gruesome, furry face with red and white eyes, snarling, sharp teeth, and pointy ears bump right at the window again and again. Piercing, yowling shrieks filled the air around the girls.

"AAAAAAHHHHHH!"

Both girls dropped to the floor and covered their eyes. They hugged each other in panic. *The creature!* She was waiting for them in the classroom. Surely she was going to come out and carry them both away to a mountain nest! They would be like the other border kids…flown away and probably eaten… never to be seen again!

They heard the door open, and too terrified to move, they now heard what sounded like a train. "SSSHHHH! Shhhhhhh!" as the shrieking continued.

Suddenly, Mimi felt a rush of hot breath on her face and felt something closing in on her... Something warm and wet touched her neck. She fainted.

Denise looked through her fingers covering her face as she trembled on the floor... There, not four feet in front of her, she saw the most beautiful boy she'd ever seen.

Chapter Three

Denise could not believe her eyes. The boy was holding a squirming, yapping bundle of commotion that she now recognized as a turbo-charged Chihuahua puppy. The Mexican boy was frantically trying to quiet his pet. "Shhhhh! Taquito, Taquito... Ssshhhhh!" he scolded. Long black hair and dark brown eyes highlighted an angelic face that seemed to have a hypnotic hold, at least for now, on Denise.

"*¿Habla Español?*" the boy whispered quietly.

Denise finally realized that she was staring at the boy with her mouth wide open. Probably not her most attractive look. Quickly trying to regain her composure, Denise stammered, "*Aaaahh....un...un poco...pero non mucho bien.*" Which was true, for as awesome as her grasp of the English language was, her grasp of the Spanish language was rudimentary, at best.

"*Mi amiga...*" Denise pointed toward Mimi, intending to

explain that Mimi spoke Spanish fluently. As she pointed, Denise suddenly realized that her friend was lying flat on her back, as if making imaginary snow angels. Denise was scared. "Mimi! Mimi!" she screamed. "Open your eyes! Please, open your eyes, please…please…please!" This didn't seem real, seeing her friend lying on her back with her eyes closed. Denise began to cry.

The boy moved close and knelt next to Mimi. He took her hand and whispered something softly. *"Esta bien, es solo mi perro."*

The Chihuahua began licking Mimi's face again while whimpering. Denise recognized the sound… Aaaaarrrrhhhh aaarrhhh-ah-ah arrHHH. *So much for the creature! Hunh! We were hearing a hyperactive Chihuahua!*

Mimi's eyes fluttered. A giant smile suddenly broke across her face and she began to giggle. She sat up, clutching the slippery, funny-looking little puppy. Denise thought, *Wow, of all the things for Mimi to see first after opening her eyes from a*

terror-induced stupor, THE best thing, without a doubt...is a puppy.
What are the odds?

Slowly but surely, everyone's thumping heartbeats, including Turbo-Chihuahua's, began to reach a reasonable rate.

The three young people made quite a sight in the middle of the sixth-floor corridor of an abandoned—probably haunted—husk of a once-glorious education building. Mimi remained on the floor, wrestling to get a grip on the little package of perpetual motion, her face getting licked like the last ice-cream cone on earth, and giggling like, well, a schoolgirl.

Just two feet away, Denise and the handsome stranger just gazed at each other like the two star-crossed sweethearts in a hundred movies. The only thing missing was violin music.

"Can someone tell me what the *heck* is going on here?" Mimi finally blurted out.

"*Me llamo Domingo. ¿Entende?*" the boy said softly.

"*Si, encantado, soy* Denise," she replied a little too eagerly, she immediately realized. "But, do you speak any English?"

"Yes, but not as good as Spanish," he stated, a little embarrassed.

"That's okay. *Esta mi amiga*, Mimi." Denise pointed to her completely preoccupied BFF. "I don't want to start trouble, but I don't think you can be in here, Domingo," she said a little hesitantly.

"Yeah!" said Mimi. "Why are you here? You scared us half to death. *¿Que pasa*, dude?"

Well, a simple *¿que pasa?* did not come with a simple answer. For at least fifteen full minutes, Domingo told his new *amigas* a spellbinding, fascinating, and terrifying tale.

As he spoke they noticed his quiet but strong demeanor, his polite manner, and especially how cute he was. He was dressed in old but clean clothes; a Texas Longhorns football jersey that was too big, coming down almost halfway to his knees, faded jeans rolled into a cuff at the bottom, and beat-up black Adidas tennis shoes.

Domingo told them that he and his mother had come to El Paso from Juarez, Mexico, two days ago. Domingo said that he lived in the southern part of Juarez, but still only about twenty miles from where they were standing.

What Domingo described was not your usual trip to El Paso, however. He lived with his mother and grandfather in the back of a small corner grocery store. His mother had been going to school, studying accounting and working part time at a local bank until about two years ago, when she was run over by a hit-and-run driver while walking home, he explained. Her hip was broken and never quite healed right, causing her to walk with a limp. She was in the hospital for a long, long time, and his grandfather Pepe had to take care of him. Pepe was the only man Domingo had ever known in his life. Domingo's mother had to quit school, she lost her bank job, and she started doing any kind of small job to support the household. Pepe was too old to work.

Her mother cleaned houses, sewed clothes, babysat, and any other modest job that she could. Domingo worked, too. He picked fruit and shined shoes whenever he could. He wasn't always able to go to school but he loved reading books and—he admitted a little timidly—writing poetry.

As Denise listened she thought of her own life and how she had never had to work, and her mother and father had always had jobs. She had always had family around like her grandmother and grandfather. She was not rich, but she had everything she needed.

She stole a glance at Mimi and could tell by her face that she was thinking the same thing. She also silently reminded herself to file away the little fact that Domingo had just disclosed about himself. *Hmmm...he likes books and reading just like me. I'm definitely going to get back to that if I get a chance.*

Domingo's story began to turn dark. He told them that his

mother grew so tired from so much work for such little money that she started listening to the many stories heard everywhere in her neighborhood about the golden opportunities in the United States. Twenty or twenty-five dollars an hour for work that she got less than five dollars for in Mexico; regular jobs with regular hours; the opportunity to go to school, to build the life that she wanted for her, her son, and her father.

One couple in particular seemed to know a way to set people up with jobs and sneak them across the border, and his mother began to meet with them. Domingo only remembered the man as being named Emilio, and he did most of the talking. The couple was older and seemed very professional and made lots of promises. Before long his mother gathered his grandfather and him in their small apartment and told them that she was going to go to the United States—to El Paso, just on the other side of the border, to work for a family. She had saved all the money she could for this chance. She said that she was going to be the maid and do some of the cooking, that she would have her own apartment, and the best part was that she could go to school at night and get her degree in accounting. Everything she had been dreaming about was there for the taking...but she had to act fast. His mother told him the chilling part...What they were going to do was illegal, and if they were caught, they could be arrested and put in jail. Domingo's mother cried and told him, "But it is the only way, *mijo*. We can't stay here! I want you to have a good life!"

Domingo's grandfather decided that he was too old and set in his ways to make any changes and told Domingo's mother to go ahead without him. He would go live with his friend. Domingo, despite being very frightened, encouraged his mother—excited to see her look so alive and energetic again.

Wow, Denise thought, *I think that's braver than I would have been*.

Domingo told them about packing a suitcase for his

mother and a backpack for himself. They were told to travel light. They cried when they said good-bye to Pepe, but he told them not to worry.

The couple showed up at the apartment and showed his mother a contract, saying that she had to sign it for anything to happen. His mother was surprised but signed the paper without really looking at it. She handed the man an envelope with all her money, which he stuffed inside his jacket. Her mind was made up and she wanted to get things moving.

The couple called someone on a cell phone and within a few minutes there was a big brown UPS truck in front of the house. The driver, wearing a UPS uniform, got out, opened the rear door, and told them to get in. It looked like the entire truck was full of boxes stacked to the ceiling. The driver grabbed a handle on one of the lower boxes and opened it like a door. Domingo saw a huge empty space behind the fake boxes. He and his mother crawled inside and, as Domingo put it, "Our lives would never be the same, again."

Denise and Mimi were on the edge of their seats, hanging on every word. They could not believe this story!

Inside the UPS van were about ten other people, all in pairs. There were three husband-and-wife couples, one brother and sister, and another mother and son.

The driver could talk to them from the front, but they were told not to talk to him. He told them not to make a sound or they could all go to jail. Domingo felt the bumps in the road pounding the beat-up truck beneath where he sat, trying not to be thrown against the other passengers. He heard whispers of *Santa Theresa*, which he knew was a border checkpoint, and *la migra*, which meant immigration officers, but he felt too paralyzed to say anything or ask questions.

Before long he felt the truck move ever so slowly under hot, glowing lights. He was half asleep but felt the truck stop and heard voices so muffled that he couldn't even tell what language they were speaking.

Denise and Mimi could see the fear in Domingo's face as

he relived his experience. He told them that he could hear the rear door to the truck open slowly. He was sure that everything was going to fall apart, that they would all be caught and sent to jail. He almost cried but he didn't want to scare his mother. He waited…eyes locked on the false cardboard door…the only thing standing between them and a life in prison. After a few minutes, he heard the door slide back down. He heard more muffled voices and then felt the truck start bumping along faster and faster. They had made it! Domingo and his mother embraced each other in silence.

The three couples were dropped off first. Then the brother and sister, and the mother and son. Domingo and his mother whispered to each other in excited anticipation. Their new start was just minutes from becoming real.

The truck stopped, the rear door screeched open, and the cardboard door was suddenly open. "Okay, last stop!" yelled the driver. Domingo and his mother stepped outside into a long empty parking lot. Domingo looked behind him and saw a familiar sight…a huge reddish brown mountain…Franklin Mountain! He had seen it every day of his life from a great distance. Except here it was ten times bigger——he was so close, he felt like he could reach out and touch it.

Domingo's mother quickly spoke up. "Where is Miss Burke? I'm supposed to go to work for her. I need to get my son to our apartment to get some rest." Without another word, the driver jumped into his truck and swerved away so fast that Domingo thought the whole thing would tip over.

As they stood in the silent darkness, Domingo looked down over a sea of lights. *This must be El Paso*, he thought. *It's beautiful!*

His thoughts were interrupted with lightning speed as a large, square black van appeared out of nowhere and stopped right beside them. The front door opened and a very big man dressed completely in black got out. "Come with me!" he growled. Without a word Domingo felt himself being grabbed from behind and put onto the floor of the truck. "Lie down and shut up!" Domingo could hear his mother saying something in protest, but could tell that she, too, was now on the floor beside him.

"Stay down! We got to get out of here quick!" he heard from the front. The man spoke in an odd-sounding manner that Domingo thought he recognized but couldn't remember from where.

Domingo was breathing so hard, he thought his lungs would explode. His mother screamed, and he heard a male voice say, "One more sound and I'll throw both of you over the side of the road. You won't stop rolling till you're back in Juarez." He laughed maniacally as the van sped along, turning and tilting madly.

When the van finally stopped, the doors were opened and Domingo and his mother were pulled out.

Domingo described the woman standing there to greet them as a woman who looked every bit as wicked as she was. Skinny, with a hatchet face, beak nose, and bright white and yellow hair. She was dressed outlandishly in a canary yellow skintight pantsuit and a light brown fur jacket. But that face! She reminded him of a legendary monster story from his childhood...La Lucheza!

At the mention of their "friend" La Lucheza, Denise and Mimi exchanged quick glances, but decided not to interrupt.

Domingo looked around quickly. They were standing before the most incredible mansion he had ever seen. The driveway snaked from a forbidding automatic iron gate, complete with guard shack, to a circular entryway in front of the house. Vast expanses of green grass, rows of hedges, duck ponds... and that was only what he could see from where he was!

"Carmella and Domingo Ventana? I have your contract here! You start in the morning!" the woman croaked in a horrible, raspy voice.

"Just a minute here!" Domingo had never seen his mother so angry. "I paid good money to get a job and an apartment here. What is the meaning of this? My son and I traveled all night, scared half to death, and then we get kidnapped and manhandled?! I thought we were going to be killed! Now I find out that *you* are the person I am supposed to be working for? Now, you're going to show us where we can put our things and get some rest. We've been traveling for a long time. And how far is the school from here?"

"You be quiet and don't say another word!" the woman screamed at the top of her lungs. "Let me explain something to you…" She started waving a few pieces of paper in front of his mother's face. "This contract makes you my employee, and you signed it. You and your son do what I say, when I say, till you pay me back. That little trip you just took cost me twenty thousand dollars. I intend to be paid back! If you wanted to go to school, you've come to the wrong place… The only thing you'll learn here is to work hard every day, and don't make trouble or else!"

"Let me see that," Domingo's mother insisted.

Domingo described a shocked look coming over his

mother's face as she silently began sobbing with her hand to her mouth.

"And before you get any ideas about breaking this contract, let me have you talk to someone." The evil woman punched in some numbers on her cell phone and said, "Hey, are you with him? Good. Put him on the line. Carmella Ventana is here with me now."

Reluctantly Domingo's mother pressed the phone to her ear. Her eyes suddenly lit up and she gasped. "Papa, are you okay? Where are you?" Silently tears began to flow down her cheeks and she sobbed, "PAPA! PAPA!"

The Evil One took the phone and barked, "Yeah, I think she gets the idea now. Keep an eye on him!" She folded the phone shut with a snap.

Two women appeared from behind the witch and motioned for the two of them to take their bags and follow. The women were older and looked at the ground, as if trying to ignore what was happening.

"Put your things away now! Work starts in three hours…
six o'clock to six o'clock is our workday around here. Kids in
sewing room A, ladies in room B. Any complaints and poor
old Papa will pay the price, and it won't be pretty! When you
sign with the Company, you *stay* with the Company, you two
got that?!" the hideous woman snarled, her grotesque face
inches from theirs, hateful spit flying from her lips with every
nasty word.

They were silently led down some stairs to a small room
with no windows, one bed, a table, a chair, and a sink. They
were pointed to a bathroom at the end of the hall. The two
women seemed to disappear, leaving them alone. Domingo
and his mother were in shock. Could this really be happening?
They had risked arrest and gave up their only relative for a
better life. Now they were far from home in a foreign country
without any papers. They could be thrown in jail if anyone
found them here. This evil witch seemed intent on working
them mercilessly. What could they do!

The girls were getting sadder and sadder listening to Domingo relive his daunting experience.

"How did you get away?" Mimi asked anxiously.

Domingo swallowed hard as if to keep from crying. "My mother is a very brave woman," he began. "She told me that we had been tricked, and bad men were holding my grandfather in Juarez. She said that if she didn't work for this awful lady, something bad would happen to Papa." Domingo was speaking almost in a whisper, looking down at his worn black shoes.

"Oh nooo!" the girls said.

Domingo said that his mother found a window high up in the bathroom. She brought the chair out of their room and was able to see outside. "Domingo, go get your backpack!" she ordered. Domingo obediently got his things, his mind racing crazily.

"*Mijo*, look at me."

Domingo reluctantly did what she asked.

"I will not have you work like a dog for these people. They are evil. I must stay here because of Papa. Don't worry about me; I can take care of myself for however long it takes. You have to run from this place. Go find Papa. Don't talk to anyone. You have to be careful so *la migra* doesn't find you. They will lock you up. Do you understand? I see a gate down at the bottom of the hill where someone as small as you should be able to squeeze through somehow. Whatever you do, keep moving until you are safe."

Domingo buried his face in his mother's warm body and squeezed her. She felt so good that he wanted to stay attached to her like that forever. "Mama, I don't want to leave you!" he croaked, unable to get the words through his sobs.

"*Mijo*, you have to save yourself for now; then we still have hope as a family," she ordered firmly. But he could see her tears, too. "Go," she hissed.

Domingo was very agile. He easily scaled the wall and went out the window. He dropped to the ground and tumbled onto his back. As he stood, he looked down a steep, grassy hill to the gate that his mother had described. Carefully but purposefully he started down the hill. He didn't see anyone within view on the right side, but thought he saw a shadow move from down the hill on his left. Suddenly he realized that a large animal was running up toward him, gathering speed as Domingo began sidestepping and going down the other side. Domingo glanced behind him and saw the white teeth of a big brown German shepherd running full speed directly at him. Domingo ran faster down the other side of the hill until he was racing full speed. As he looked over his shoulder, he saw the black shape of the guard dog now running down the hill straight for him! His mind told his legs to go faster, but he already knew that this was faster than he had ever run. The dog was getting closer, and Domingo could hear fierce, menacing growls. He saw the gate near the bottom of the hill and, indeed, there were a couple of inches between the stone pillar and the iron gate where he could possibly squeeze through.

That didn't matter for now, though. The dog was closing in, and Domingo, exhausted, thought of his mother watching from the window. *I have to get away from here; I have to keep my mother hoping. I have to think!*

Suddenly he saw a duck pond, not very big, but the white flowers of the lily pads caught his eye. A short bench sat in front of the pond, which was about thirty feet to the right of the gate.

An idea flashed into Domingo's head. He gathered all the energy he had and raced directly at the wooden bench. The dog was so close now that Domingo could almost feel his breath. With all his might, Domingo launched himself, planting his right foot on the bench and pushing with every ounce of strength he could gather. With the speed from the hill and the bounce from the jump, Domingo soared close to twenty feet in the air before landing on the other side of the duck pond. The German shepherd, so close to his prey, eyes white with anticipation, suddenly found himself tumbling and splashing totally out of control in a dizzying water crash.

Domingo rolled a few times and came to a stop. He knew he had to act fast. He raced to the gate and saw that it was made of black metal bars like a prison, but the bar nearest the stone wall was a little loose. He squirmed his body through so his legs and hips were on the outside, but his head and backpack got stuck. As Domingo struggled he could hear the guard dog sloshing out of the water. He flattened the backpack and pushed it through the bottom half of the gate. His head throbbed as he pulled it against the iron gate and the stone wall. All the running at maximum speed had caused him to sweat heavily, and it saved him now; he slipped from the gate and into freedom with one final buck. He dropped to his knees, exhausted, his head pounding. He glanced up and met the panting gaze of his opponent, still growling. "*Perro*, you were fast. But today I was smarter." Domingo heard a man's voice from the darkness behind the defeated German shepherd. "Major! Major! What have you got there, boy?" Domingo recognized the voice. It was deep and rough and had the same scary accent—the driver! He now recognized the accent as Arnold Schwarzenegger's in the movie *The Terminator*.

Domingo told the girls that he took one last glance at the huge mansion holding his mother and who knows how many others, and set out to figure out some kind of plan.

He told them that as he looked over El Paso in the early morning moonlight, one glorious steeple on a beautiful adobe-yellow chapel stood out far below him. He didn't know why, but he felt in his heart that the building was calling to him. Somehow it would give him the answers he needed to get his mother and grandfather back. After a long, long walk down through the empty city streets, he finally reached the building and found himself on the Santa Maria Academy campus, staring at their impressive chapel. Domingo explained feeling a certain peace and comfort on the spacious grounds.

He was totally exhausted but had just enough energy to search for a hiding place as daylight broke... He found an unlocked door in the basement of this abandoned building and walked up and down each corridor until he saw the cases of water and supplies stashed in room 606. That door, too, miraculously, was unlocked, so he stayed there. He rearranged some boxes to hide himself and make a little room.

Denise and Mimi were shocked. "I can't believe this!" Denise exclaimed. "People can't just keep other people and make them work! There's laws against that!"

"Yeah!" echoed Mimi. "We're not going to let them get away with this!"

"No, no, no!" cried Domingo. "This is my problem. We can't let anyone know about this, or my grandfather will be in danger. I must obey my mother's wishes."

"Then, why aren't you back in Mexico?" Denise asked.

"Well, I'm trying to think of a way to save my mother and my grandfather. He is in danger, too. He can't help me!" Domingo replied. "We don't have anyone! There must be *someone, somewhere...*"

After an extremely brief BFF glance—a quick nonverbal exchange—Denise blurted out, "You've got us. I'm a detective!

Well…my father and I are detectives. He's found thousands of people all over the country; he's even been on TV. If we put our minds to it and use our heads, we can find your mom!"

"Yeah!" Mimi chimed in. "We can figure things out; that's what we do, and we're really good at it! And you'll be surprised; we're not scared of anything!"

Domingo had to admit these girls had the spirit and energy that he was going to need if he was going to succeed in this ginormous and seemingly impossible operation.

"Hey! How long have we been up here? They're gonna think we ran away or got lost or skipped school or something," Denise suddenly remembered. "Quick, put four boxes of the hand sanitizer on the cart and let's get back!"

Domingo knew exactly where everything was in his new *casa*, so he loaded the girls up and got them on the elevator. The girls swatted the dust off their uniforms as they got in.

"Hey, where did Taquito come from? He wasn't part of the story," Mimi asked on the way down.

Domingo chuckled. "The first day I was here, I smelled food and snuck over near the cafeteria. As I got close, I saw the little *perro* running with something in his mouth and a skinny lady wearing an apron chasing him and yelling."

"Mrs. C!" The BFFs chuckled as they thought of their friendly lunch lady chasing a Chihuahua. Too bad they didn't have a video. *America's Funniest Home Videos* would have loved it!

"I saw that he was hiding right near the basement door that I used to get in, and he was stealing tacos and stashing them. I called him Little Taco or *Taquito*. He started following me and has been with me ever since. Except now I think he has a new best friend."

Mimi giggled; she had not put the puppy down since being "attacked" into unconsciousness. "Puppies and I are like peanut butter and jelly." She laughed. "My one request if we're going to work together is that Taquito and I are partners."

"Okay, done," Denise and Domingo answered in embarrassingly perfect harmony. They looked at each other and giggled nervously.

"That means *you two* are also partners!" Mimi squealed.

Denise could feel her cheeks turning red.

As Domingo pushed the supplies to the front door, he turned serious again. "Please don't tell anyone about this. I trust you two, but I don't want anything to happen to my mother or grandfather. Let's try to figure something out."

"Your secret is safe, Domingo," Denise tried to assure him, "but don't forget. You are in the United States. Things are different here. We can help you. We just don't know how yet. We'll be back."

Domingo cradled Taquito as he stared at the friends pushing the loaded-down cart together. He couldn't help but be impressed at their ability to work together as they steered the load over the winding cement trail. "Taquito, these two funny little ones seem to have enough spirit for ten people. Let's hope they're smart enough and brave enough to help us. I miss my mother so much that it hurts."

The little Chihuahua looked up at him and blinked.

Chapter Four

"Sorry, Mrs. Caramia! That old elevator was so slow it took us forever. But here is the magic potion!" Denise announced when they finally returned to the classroom.

"Oh, my goodness! I was worried sick about you two! I was just about to have Mrs. England go up there to find you."

"No, no, no, don't do that!" Mimi cried. "There's no reason to go up there!"

Mrs. Caramia seemed startled. "Okay, Mimi, relax. I was just concerned about you guys."

"We're fine…no problems," Denise added, taking her seat.

The weekend homework assignments were given out and class was dismissed before Denise and her friend had a chance to think too much about their eventful mission-turned-adventure.

They huddled at their usual spot—a picnic table under a tree near the cafeteria loading dock.

"Let's think about this," Denise began. "I think we should outline it like a homework problem. My father always makes a list of people we have to talk to and places we have to go to start gathering all the information we're gonna need, got it?"

"Well, I guess..." Mimi's voice trailed off. "Are you really sure we can do something here? We're just kids, and he doesn't want us to tell anyone. How are we gonna talk to people and go to places? El Paso is a huge city."

"No one said it would be easy," Denise told her. "We're going to have to get creative...in fact, maybe tell a fib here or there. You saw how desperate that boy looked, Meems. If we don't help him, no one will. Come on. It's worth the risk to keep this family together. How would we feel if something like this happened to one of us and there was no one to turn to?"

Denise's gaze wandered to the old high school building

staring down at her with its window eyes. She was sure that she could feel a pair of dark brown human eyes staring hopefully at her. It made her feel good to know that someone was counting on her; she really loved helping people. She also knew this was not a simple problem to try to solve.

"Hey, Niecy! Have fun at school today?" A voice broke her daydream.

"Yes, Daddy," she dutifully replied, directing her attention to her father, typically dressed in his Boston Red Sox shirt and jeans.

"No, you didn't," answered her father, completing their daily after-school routine. Her father thought it was hilarious; she merely tolerated it.

Dennis Lawson was a retired San Francisco Police captain who loved puns and word play, a trait Denise had obviously inherited. He also *loved* his Boston sports teams, for that is where he actually grew up. Now that he was retired, he spent a lot of his time dropping off and picking up his daughter and son and accompanying them to their after-school activities. During the days he ran his investigations business and was trying his hand at writing.

Jacob was skipping five feet in front of his father as they crossed the schoolyard. "Tag! You're it!" Jacob suddenly slapped his father's belly and began running away. Seeing the sudden burst of motion, Denise and Mimi automatically joined in. They loved playing tag with the onetime detective. He was a devoted CrossFit enthusiast, sturdily built, so he was in good enough shape to play a long game... However... he had a lot of years on him, and speed was never his strongest attribute. The kids loved to tease him by letting him get thiiiisss close before darting away just out of his grasp. Being a good sport, he diligently chased until he had to surrender in exhaustion. Jacob usually livened up the games by giving his father a few "funny" insults about the ever-widening bald spot that occupied the top of his head. Usually a good time was had by all.

"Daddy, can I go over to Mimi's house? We're working on a new project, and we're gonna have to make a presentation."

Denise shot Mimi a sideways glance and nodded her head.

"Mimi, did your mom say it was okay?" Mr. Lawson asked.

"Yeah, of course, it's only for a few hours," Mimi stammered, taking the hint, but nervous about fibbing.

Mr. Lawson knew where Mimi lived. It was only four short blocks away. The kids piled into the big dark Sequoia, and Jacob buckled into his booster. In the few short minutes that the girls had, Mimi texted her mother. "Going over Denise's to work on project. OK? TTYL Smiley Face. Mimi." Within seconds she got a response. "No prob. Do u need a ride?"

Mimi quickly responded, "Denise's dad," just as they pulled to the front of her house.

"Niecey, I'll be back in two hours. That's 5:30. Understand? It's Friday, traffic's going to be bad, don't be late!"

"Yes, Daddy!" Denise groaned impatiently. "We'll be done by then. See you later. Love you!"

The girls walked inside the gate and walked about five steps. Mimi said out of the corner of her mouth, not moving her head, "Is he gone?"

"Yep, give it another second though. Okay, come on!" They stashed their backpacks under the porch and set out.

They quickly retraced their steps and headed right back to their school, hearts thumping. They were entering that zone of adventure where they knew they were doing something they weren't supposed to, but the opportunity was too exciting to pass up.

The campus was quiet, almost deserted, when they arrived. Domingo had been watching from his room and waved to get their attention. Denise pointed to the front door, motioning for him to come down. The three now-partners met at the door, taking care that no one saw. They quickly slipped inside. Taquito jumped into Mimi's arms while Domingo and Denise smiled at each other awkwardly.

"Domingo, my father always says that you have to go to

the crime scene to figure out what the criminal is thinking and how he committed the crime. You have to be able to understand what happened and how. That means we have to find the house where they brought you and your mom," Denise said. "You said you looked down and saw the tall tower and the chapel. Can you tell us like, what the angle was, and about how far you think it was?"

Domingo appeared embarrassed. "What is an angle?" he asked.

"Well…" Denise stooped down and drew a rectangle in the dust on the floor with her finger. "Say this is the chapel and the tower." She reached into her uniform pocket and took out what looked like a regular silver pen. When she grabbed one of the ends and pulled, it stretched out into a long, skinny rod.

"What in the world is that thing?" Mimi demanded incredulously.

"My grandfather made it for me. It's one of his inventions.

Look, there's a grabber thing on the end so you can pick things up without bending down." As she spoke she tried to pick up an old pencil stub from the floor. The pencil fell as soon as she picked it up.

"Oh well, back to the drawing board." Mimi chuckled. She had seen quite a few of these odd little inventions, and they almost all ended up with the same results.

"Well, look, I can still use it for a pointer." Denise said with a chuckle.

She turned her attention back to Domingo. He was studying the diagram and nodding.

"Remember looking down...what part of the building was closest to you?"

"Ooh, I see, yes, yes. I would say this corner right here." He pointed to the left front corner near where the main entrance would be.

"Okay, now, how far do you think you walked that night? I know you were thinking about a lot of things, but could you guess? How many streets did you pass? Did you see any stores? We need to know things like that."

"I remember walking down a long hill for quite a distance. When I got to flatter streets, I remember a gas station that was closed. It was difficult to see the chapel, so I made many wrong turns and wasted much time. Somehow I made it. It seemed like more than an hour, maybe even two."

"That's a good start. The only problem is that we've only got two hours to figure this out and get back to Mimi's," Denise declared. "Meems, can you and Taquito pay attention? We need everybody on this mission. Pull out your phone and go to Google Earth."

Mimi smiled admiringly. She loved when Denise got in this problem-solving mode…it brought out her confident side. If there was one thing that baffled Mimi about Denise, it was her reaction to anything negative. It didn't take much for Denise to go into a funk if someone embarrassed or teased her.

Mimi quickly pulled her iPhone 5S from its pink Monster High case and began finger-jabbing the screen. Domingo's eyes grew big and he gasped, "Is that your phone?"

"Yes!" snapped Mimi defensively, wondering if this boy was trying to be sarcastic, dissing her phone.

"But you are only nine years old!" he declared incredulously. "Where did you get it?"

"My mother gave it to me for my birthday," Mimi answered. She could tell by the look on his face that this was a totally foreign concept to him. She felt a little guilty about assuming that he possibly had a better phone than she did.

"At least half the class has iPhones. I'm going to get one for doing so well in the spelling bee!" Denise added casually. "...at least I hope!"

"In my neighborhood, only some of the grownups have cell phones and not usually fancy ones like that," Domingo responded.

The girls suddenly felt embarrassed for Domingo and also

for themselves…the truth was, they had never actually met anyone who didn't have working parents, a home, cars, and nice things.

This made Denise even more motivated. "Mimi, enter Santa Maria Academy in Google Earth. When it comes up move the cursor toward the mountain and we can see what houses have a lot of land and duck ponds. While you're at it, Google 'The Company' and see what that's all about." She paused for breath. "Domingo, we need to have a reason to be going door-to-door in these neighborhoods. Was there anything in the storage room, a.k.a. your new home, that we could use to make it look like we're selling things for, like, a fundraiser? God knows they make us do those stupid things enough for real!"

"I have the perfect idea!" cried Domingo. "But I need some help."

"Lead the way!" Denise ordered merrily. This reminded her of the investigations that she and her father worked on.

They would spend a lot of time doing the boring stuff like getting information and doing research...but then suddenly her father would come up with the plan. He would name off the steps they needed to take in rapid-fire order, much like Denise had just done with her friends. Denise felt the same kind of excitement and anticipation that she had seen light up her father's face so many times.

Domingo brought her up to the storage room, where he showed her two cardboard boxes of chocolate bars that she recognized from one of last year's fundraisers. She couldn't remember the cause. "This will work perfectly!" she exclaimed. They each grabbed a box and headed back to the elevator.

Denise applied a brand-new layer of lip gloss, this time raspberry, and started prodding this mystery boy. Her father had taught her that it is easy to get people to talk about themselves if you flatter them and show interest. Of course in this case, she really was interested.

"So, what kind of books do you like?" she asked, just a little shyly.

"Actually, I like poetry the most. I know that might sound strange coming from a boy my age, but it's always made me feel like I am inside someone else's thoughts for a short time. I find that feeling very relaxing and...how do you say...*satisfacer?*"

"Satisfying. Yeah...I feel that way when I read books... It's like you connect with the author and go through the experience together."

"*Si, si, si!*" Domingo was smiling broadly. "I would like to write poetry someday."

"Oh, I bet you will. I'm going to be an author someday."

The elevator let them off, and they eagerly resumed their planning stage.

Outside, Mimi breathlessly exclaimed, "From what Domingo described, I can see a whole row of big homes with lots of grass, and two have duck ponds! The closest street is called Red Mountain Drive!" Taquito yipped his agreement.

"Okay, we've got less than two hours to get up there, snoop around, and see if we can figure out where Domingo's mom is. Let's go!"

"Anything on 'the company,' Meems?" Denise asked as they started out.

"Nah, too many matches. We need more info."

They walked quickly, none of them willing to admit that they weren't really sure if this was a great idea. No one wanted to be the first one to let the others know about the uneasy, dancing butterflies racing in their stomachs. It was a strange mix of fear, excitement, and wonder. One look at the faces of the three young heroes made it obvious that the feeling was contagious.

They passed a gas station, and within a few blocks the sidewalks began to steepen, making their boxes heavy. They kept switching off so one of them could rest at a time. It felt Sooo good to rest!

"Uh, oh..." Mimi whispered, "I think that's Jimmy Cavanaugh on his bike up there."

Denise peered up the street at a large round form riding an impossibly small bicycle. It reminded her of a circus bear she had seen last year at the Coliseum. "Of all the people..." she responded. "Be cool, you guys, I'll do the talking."

Jimmy was a classmate of the girls. Mystery and myth surrounded him. Rumors from his early years had it that Jimmy was born without bones and consisted only of a body of skin that had to be filled to the max at all times to avoid becoming deflated. Denise never believed such a fantastic tale, but upon close examination, he did seem to be just a large round ball. Kids claimed to have seen Jimmy's mother feeding him bowls of pudding with a little shovel to make sure he kept his shape. Thus was born one of El Paso's most unfortunate but fitting nicknames: Jimmy the Pudding Boy.

Strangely, Jimmy also was a kid who could acquire things that other kids needed. He was a sort of a junior problem solver around his neighborhood.

"Hey, Jimmy, what's up?" Denise hailed.

Jimmy straddled his tiny bike, eyed them suspiciously, and demanded, "What are you guys doing up here? You don't live here! And where did you get the big rat?"

Mimi cradled Taquito while she glared at the Pudding Boy, but she held her tongue.

"We're going door to door for a fundraiser. That's Mimi's cousin; he's just helping." Denise nodded her head toward Domingo.

"There's no fundraiser going on right now, and how come you guys are alone? This isn't your neighborhood," Jimmy repeated accusingly.

Denise had a bolt of an idea. "Aw, Jimmy, you're too smart for us. You're right, there's no fundraiser," she whispered confidentially. "This kid's Mimi's neighbor. He gets these boxes of chocolate from his father's store. We sell them and split the money. Listen, you don't want to wreck a good thing, do you? How about we give you a couple of bars and you don't tell anyone…what do you say?"

SOMEONE, SOMEWHERE

Jimmy's ears perked up at the mention of chocolate. "Make it five and we got a deal!" he barked.

"Done! Domingo! *Cinco por mi amigo, por favor.*" Denise shifted again to her conspirator tone. "Hey, Jimmy, you live here... Is there a big house, lot of land, duck ponds with a guard dog....maybe a lady with white and yellow hair?"

"Are you kidding?" Jimmy scoffed. "All these places are two hundred feet from the street; they all have walls and gates! They're not the kind of people who walk around making small talk with kids. When I go door to door, the closest I get is the guard shack or the front gate! I stuck my nose too close to a fence once and a dog almost bit it!"

The friends exchanged quick looks of encouragement.

"What kind of dog?" asked Mimi.

"They all have different ones, and they're all ferocious! Supposedly a kid got his arm bitten off by a German shepherd a couple of years ago. And the dog ate it!"

"Whereabouts was that place?" Denise asked casually, zeroing in on the news of a German shepherd...

"That street up there." Jimmy pointed. "The higher up this mountain you go, the bigger the houses and the meaner the dogs."

The group looked about half a block from where they stood. Mimi squinted to read the street sign: Red Mountain Road!

Just then a big brown UPS truck roared by them and quickly turned right. Domingo's blood ran cold and he thought his legs would collapse. Suddenly fear was pushing his courage and hope aside. He took several deep breaths and closed his eyes. Was this really happening?

Denise looked back over her shoulder and could see the tower of Santa Maria. It was just as Domingo described. Once more, she felt the warm stab in her belly that told her this was the time to act.

Instinct! They were close! It's here somewhere!

"Let's move!" she cried.

They raced to the corner, turned right, and arrived just in time to see the red lights on the back of the UPS truck as it slid through the automatic gate to the biggest house that any of them had ever seen.

"Is that the place, Domingo?" Denise panted.

"I only saw it for a minute in the dark...I'm not sure..." he murmured haltingly.

"It's got to be it!" Denise declared. By now they were standing right next to the gate, which had swung shut automatically. The numbers 1-1-6-1 were affixed to the column beside the gate. A stone wall with what looked like a ten-foot-high black fence ran imposingly for half the block, successfully communicating the subtle message "Hey, No One Is Welcome Here! This Means You!"

One of Denise's spelling bee words popped into her head: o-m-i-n-o-u-s.

Despite being pretty far from the house, they could hear

doors opening and closing, work being done, and a few shouts in men's voices. Denise thought that one of the voices sounded German. She remembered the accents of the bad soldiers in *The Sound of Music*. It was her mother's favorite movie, and it was not lost on Denise that there were young kids in danger during the escape scene of that movie. This was no movie, though. She fought to control her brain, which was frantically telling her to turn back.

"Hey, Domingo, I think I heard Arnold Schwarzenegger," Denise teased, trying to lighten the mood.

"Ha, ha." They both laughed sarcastically.

Suddenly, the big gate swung open from inside. As it slowly hinged all the way open, they instinctively moved to one side with their backs stuck right up to the wall, trying to make themselves invisible and silent, like part of the wall itself.

The UPS truck bounced along, gaining speed, and turned back down the way it came. The driver never even looked their way.

"Wheeewww!" they sighed in unison.

The gate was noiselessly swinging shut, like giant scissors. Denise cried, "Come on, now's our chance!"

Seeing her two accomplices paralyzed by their fear, she sprang into action. With one hand she pushed Domingo from the back and with the other she pulled Mimi by the hand. Denise was not very big, but her gymnastics training and keeping up with her little brother had given her deceptive muscle power.

Like a clumsy six-legged beast, the three of them managed to get inside the gate seconds before it clanged shut. They stopped and stared at one another in total, stunned silence, ducking down behind some hedges.

"Denise, I'm scared. What do we do now?" Mimi was starting to sob.

Denise saw that her friend was about to lose her nerve. Her father had told her during their investigations that there will always be certain points where you have to make decisions and choices. He always said to try to stick with the plan and to remember the mission. Denise knew that even though they were all scared, this was their chance to find out what was going on in this creepy place. She swallowed hard and pushed herself forward.

"You guys take the candy and go to the front door," Denise ordered. "Domingo, if the witch is there, do you think she'll remember you?"

"It's hard to say," he replied, eyes wide open. "She only talked to my mother."

"Well, if she says anything, run back down to this gate. See that button there? That's how you open it. But, listen, we all have to be brave and act normal. Nobody is gonna think that kids are really detectives," Denise rationalized with her reluctant but determined partners.

"What about you?" Domingo asked anxiously. "Aren't you coming with us?"

"I'm going to look around and see if I can figure out what kind of shenanigans are going on in this mansion of horrors."

"Shenanigans" was one of Denise's favorite words, but it barely registered with her now with things happening so fast.

"You see anything?" she asked Domingo, who was just tall enough to peek over the hedge.

"The guard with the dog is driving away in a golf cart. No one is near the house," he whispered excitedly.

"Let's try to meet back here in about fifteen minutes!" Denise ducked low and slipped through a narrow gap in the bushes.

Domingo and Mimi stared at each other in shocked silence. Taquito gave a little yip as if to encourage them. "You're right, Taquito! If Denise can do this, so can we! Ready, Domingo?"

"*Si, estoy listo*! I'm ready!" he said confidently. Gathering himself, he began to stride toward the house that had been the start of his three-day ordeal. He felt angry and afraid, but strangely protected.

Denise was awestruck by the sheer size of the house. Half brick, half wood, two stories high, the house had rounded tower-like shapes on all four corners. Pointed roofs covered the towers. Denise scanned the front side of the house as she stayed behind the hedge line. She saw a small sign that said "Deliveries" with an arrow pointing to her left. She tiptoed through a long garden of beautiful but forbidding cactus plants, careful not to rub up against the treacherous spines. She had made that mistake once before, when she first moved to this desert town. She had reached to grab one and had ended up screaming in pain with the needles stuck in her hand. Her father jokingly called them "our friend, the cactus" ever since.

She reached the corner of the house and noticed a stairwell leading down to a door a few feet down the wall. She could see some sort of outdoor elevator coming up from the driveway. She remembered seeing these kinds of elevators in San Francisco near the department stores. Every Christmas her family would go downtown to shop and see the lights. She was so amazed at the incredible numbers of people crushing against one another, but she also marveled at the vendors, cab drivers, and deliverymen who had to weave their way through the mobs of people every day.

Lined up next to the elevator were two carts, loaded to overflowing with cloth and fabric. The carts had soft canvas sides like baskets and were about half the size of a sofa.

As Denise watched cautiously, she saw two women ride up the elevator, load a cart onto the platform, and disappear back down below the pavement. Denise could not help but notice the sadness in the women's expressions. They stared down toward the ground and did not speak with each other.

Denise seized on a risky idea and made a dash for the last basket. As she got close she could hear the mechanical hum of the motor pulling the elevator back up. With a nimble hop she jumped into the basket and quickly covered herself with the cloth, burrowing into the soft stuff like a big gopher.

Denise didn't dare move a muscle as she heard the metallic bump of the elevator coming to a stop. Within seconds she felt herself moving along inside the basket. Onto the platform, and then—a sudden downward plunge which she felt in the pit of her stomach. She was inside the horror house!

Strangely, she was too excited about getting away with her plan to be scared. Of course the bad news was that her plan didn't go any further. She was a good improviser though, so she felt fully alert and ready for anything!

The elevator stopped and Denise felt the basket roll a short distance before bumping into something with a dull thud… then silence and stillness. She sensed that the two sad ladies had left the basket and walked away.

Denise slowly, slowly, slowly poked her head up to see where she was. A dimly lit hallway held the other basket of fabric, a set of clothes hooks where she could see a few white smocks hanging, and a pretty Mexican woman…looking right in her eyes!

It was hard to tell who was more shocked, as the woman's eyes were open almost as wide as her mouth. Denise held her finger to her lips, hoping by some miracle that the woman would not betray her. The woman quickly averted her eyes and walked halfway down the hall and disappeared through a doorway. Denise couldn't help but notice the woman's intelligent eyes and smooth skin with a small beauty mark on her cheek. She also noticed that she favored her right leg just slightly but enough so you could tell. Tightly wrapping her dark hair was a beautiful red and gold scarf. The woman was wearing a white smock like the ones hanging.

Denise got out of the basket, found a small smock and put it on. She tiptoed to the doorway. The air in the hallway was hot and stifling, and she could hear a racket of machinery from another room. She tasted steam in the heavy air as she peered through the doorway into a huge space about the size of the school gym. Rows of large sewing machines lined the left side, with women pushing pieces of cloth through, like the cloth she had just been immersed in.

Looking to the right, Denise could not believe her eyes. Six kids—who looked a little older than she was, but not by much—were also working. Some were cutting the cloth with large scissors, while others were folding shirts. One girl was hanging dresses on large rolling clothes racks like the ones Denise remembered seeing in Macy's.

Denise was spellbound...she stood and gawked at the scene. She had never seen anything like this before. The noise and smells were overpowering.

It's true! she thought. What the woman had told Domingo was true. These women and children were working away for her. And now Denise could see what they did. They were making clothes! Which, she was sure, the lady was selling. This was a little clothing factory! Denise was blown away.

Absentmindedly, Denise wandered onto the floor, passing through the doorway and taking a few steps toward the woman she had seen, who was working on the machine closest to the door, but looking right at Denise. Before Denise could say anything, the woman gave her an alarmed look and shook her head quickly. Denise stopped in her tracks. The woman silently but firmly nodded her head upward and directed her eyes to the wall directly behind the junior sleuth. Only then did Denise notice a large glass window on the wall above the entryway. She had almost broken one of her father's rules of caution…always look before entering or exiting a place of business: You don't want to walk in on a robbery.

She backed up and hugged the wall. She heard a man's deep voice with a foreign accent boom, "Who's there? Is someone down there?" Denise's heart felt like it was going to blow up. She could hear rapid footsteps on wooden steps. THUMP, THUMP, THUMP, THUMP, THUMP…

With no time to run, Denise had to think fast. She noticed one of the rolling clothes racks full of colorful dresses a few feet to her right. Without thinking she walked over, grabbed the crossbar, and did a pull-up just like in gymnastics. All those core conditioning sessions that her coach loved and she hated were coming in handy now as she turned upside down and hooked her legs over the bar with her knees. Hanging still, she gathered the dresses close and didn't move a muscle.

"Did you see someone come in here?" insisted a booming voice. Denise now recognized the voice as Arnold Schwarzenegger. She could feel him pacing back and forth, looking for anything out of place. "I could have sworn I saw something!"

Denise was petrified, and hanging upside down, she felt a slow trickle of sweat start to run down her back. It tickled like crazy, even though there was nothing funny about her situation. She held her breath and thought for sure that she couldn't hang on and keep from panicking at the same time. While she hung like a giant bat, her eyes fell on a curious sight. In a shallow basket on a table near the dress rack she could see several cloth labels like the ones that attached to the neck part of clothes. The labels read, "American Justice."

"*No, señor, no es nada.* No one is here." Denise heard a soft voice from the machine where she knew the woman was working.

"*Nada*, huh?" the man said skeptically. "Well, if I see any funny business, all of you will pay! Understand?!"

"*Si, señor, entendo.* I understand."

Denise thought she would burst from not being able to scratch the tickle, but she held on till she heard the footsteps pound back upstairs. Denise reached up, grabbed the bar, and spun herself down. She backed up to the doorway and found a corner. She ground against it, purring to herself as she itched her back where the sweat had been slowly torturing her. She felt like she had been trapped upside down for hours, and she knew she had to get out of this dangerous situation right now.

A little voice arose in Denise's mind, telling her that she was forgetting something…maybe she was leaving something out…*Aha!…I know what it is!* Another one of her father's detective lessons. It's not what you know; it's what you can show!

Denise eyed the basket of designer labels near the dress rack. She looked up toward where the shop window overlooked the factory floor. Could she risk grabbing a label without being seen? That would blow her whole mission. She thought for a few seconds, then smiled to herself slowly. *I think I have the perfect solution.*

The woman glanced at her while keeping her head down. Denise silently retrieved her grandfather's cockamamie invention from her pocket, extended it to its full length, and reached for a label. She strained and stretched with every fiber of her arms and shoulders, keeping out of view of the ever-vigilant and totally nasty guard.

Another half inch…*Yessss!* This time it worked like a charm. The grabber had grabbed! She pocketed the label and collapsed the grabber. *Hey! That's what I can name this new invention, The Grabber! But, for now, time to make an escape!*

She made eye contact with the woman, mouthed, "Thank you," and re-entered the hallway. She hung the smock where she had found it and saw a staircase right beside the elevator. She walked up one flight and saw a wooden door with a glass window, covered by a metal grate. Carefully she looked outside. It led to where she had gotten onto the elevator, and she couldn't see anyone. She opened the door carefully and slid outside. Then she shut the door without making a sound and ran back to the hedges that led to the driveway.

Her mind was so full of thoughts that Denise could not concentrate on anything. She knew she and her friends had to get away from this place, though. She forced herself to stop, take a deep breath, and focus on what to do next. She immediately thought of her friends and began to walk around to where the front door was located. She wasn't even close when she heard a horrible, piercing woman's voice shrieking, "If you kids ever come onto this property again, I won't bother to call the cops. I'll just sic the dogs on you. See how you like that!"

Quick footsteps sounded from up the driveway. Denise saw Mimi, holding Taquito, and Domingo, holding the boxes of chocolate, running toward her with petrified looks on their faces. Seeing her friends' terror angered Denise beyond words.

What kind of evil people were these? she wondered. This had to be stopped, and they had to be punished for treating people so maliciously. Yes, "maliciously" was an interesting word, but she was not thinking that way right now. She was angry, and more determined than ever.

She joined her friends and together they reached the controls for the gate. "Don't say anything, just go!" Denise commanded. Domingo pushed the big button and the gate swung open. All three scrambled out onto the street with a collective sigh of relief.

"Oh my gosh, oh my gosh, oh my gosh!" Denise gushed. "You guys are not gonna believe what I saw. Keep moving, we can't stop here!"

As they fast-walked, Denise excitedly told her friends about seeing the dress shop set up inside the house, all the women and kids working away, the American Justice labels, and of course, Arnold Schwarzenegger almost catching her. "Thank goodness for that nice lady," Denise babbled. "You know, it's funny, but right away I noticed the most beautiful scarf, red and gold. Somehow I knew she was kind and I could trust her."

"Red and gold scarf?" gasped Domingo. "What did she look like?" Denise described the pretty woman with the beauty mark and distinctive walk. Domingo's face brightened. "That was my mama!" he cried joyfully.

Denise thought he was going to cry, but he quickly got control of himself. She suddenly realized that Mimi hadn't said a word. "What happened at the door, Mimi?"

Mimi was hugging Taquito harder than usual. Denise could see that she was shaken up. Voice quivering, she started to speak. "Well, we saw these giant double doors that looked like they were to a museum. I got really scared, but I went ahead and rang the doorbell. Two ladies answered wearing maid outfits. It was really weird; they wouldn't look us in the eye, and they spoke so softly we could hardly hear them.

"We said we were selling candy to raise money for our school...but before we could finish they told us that they weren't allowed to buy anything. One of them said, 'You must leave... now!' She seemed really scared. Domingo asked her what kind of place this was, like a museum or what? One of the ladies said, 'This is The Company.' When I asked, 'What company?' all of a sudden we heard this hideous screaming from somewhere upstairs... 'Who's asking all those questions?! Who came to this door? I've told you two, no one is allowed in this house!'

"We could hear the lady coming down the stairs, and it was getting louder. The two ladies at the door said, 'Go! Now!' and we did. We never saw the lady on the stairs, but I'll never forget that voice. Denise, this is scary...those are really bad people, and there's something creepy going on in there."

Denise suddenly felt bad for sending Mimi into such a crazy situation. She didn't blame her for being scared. She wrapped her arms around her BFF, careful not to smoosh Taquito, and whispered to her, "You're my BFF, Meems, and you were really brave. Let's get home and we can figure out what to do next."

They continued walking really fast. The trip back to Mimi's would be almost all downhill. Though lost in thought and trying to control her own emotions, Denise now looked at Domingo. She could not even imagine how she would feel if her mother or brother were in any type of danger. "Hey, at least we know where she is and that she's okay," Denise said. "We've got to figure out what we can do about it."

"What can we do?" Domingo asked. "The lady has the paper and they will hurt my grandpa if anything goes wrong. We are helpless...we are just children!" His voice was getting higher and Denise thought that he would cry, but he somehow steadied himself. "Maybe I should go back and work with her so we can at least be together."

"Domingo, no!" the girls cried in unison.

"They can't get away with this!" Denise exclaimed. "I'm not sure, but it doesn't seem legal to make someone work in a place they don't want to. Just because they signed a contract!" She exaggerated the word "contract" mockingly, and made fake quotation marks with her fingers like it was some huge deal. "But, listen. First things first. Mimi, how much time do we have to get back to your house?"

"Oh!" Mimi gulped. "We've only got twenty minutes; we'll never make it!"

Half a block ahead Denise spotted the distinctive basketball shape of Jimmy the Pudding Boy. She hustled to get closer. "Hey, Jimmy! Come here a second!"

Jimmy pedaled his bike up to the trio, eying them suspiciously once again. "Where've you guys been? You look like you've seen a ghost!"

"You wouldn't believe it if we told you, Jimmy," Denise replied. "Just as you said, nobody wanted anything to do with our fake fundraiser. But I have a proposition for you."

Mimi, Domingo, and Taquito watched as Denise sidled up to Jimmy and whispered something in his ear. They could see the lights of Jimmy's brain come to life and brighten up his face slowly. He nodded quickly and pedaled off.

Denise turned to her friends and said, "Come on. He's gonna meet us at the corner."

The partners dutifully followed Denise to the corner. Within a minute Jimmy pedaled back into view. He was holding something across his handle bars.

"Okay, let's do it!" Jimmy cried out. He braked to a stop and placed two skateboards at their feet.

"A deal's a deal!" declared Denise. She took the two boxes of chocolate from Domingo and gave them to Jimmy. "We'll leave your stuff in Mimi's yard; you can pick it up whenever your dad gets home! Come on, you guys!"

With that Denise got on one of the skateboards. Without missing a beat, Mimi got on the bike and Domingo got on the other skateboard.

Domingo and Denise took turns hanging onto the bike and free-wheeling, and Mimi just tried to keep the bike heading downhill, which really wasn't easy with Taquito stuffed under her shirt. With no helmets or pads, they knew that if they fell, it would be a disaster. Considering what they'd already been through that day, though, it didn't seem like that big of a deal.

First stop was Santa Maria, where they said good-bye and good night to Domingo. They took his skateboard and made it to Mimi's house at exactly 5:28. Could they have cut it any closer?

Chapter Five

The girls hung back on the sidewalk and almost immediately saw the familiar gray Sequoia slow to a stop in front of the house. "Hey, Mimi," Mr. Lawson sang. "You kids have fun?"

"Yes," they said in a monotone...because they felt they had to.

"No, you didn't," replied Mr. Lawson cheerfully, chuckling. Denise marveled to herself, *Boy, he sure likes to chuckle.*

On the drive home, Mr. Lawson asked, "Hey, Niecey, did you get your project done?"

"Hmm...some of it. We still have work to do." She didn't feel good about lying to her father, but she was still trying to sort out her plan.

"What's it about?" he asked eagerly.

"Oh...it's about different kinds of sharks." She did intend

to do a project like that, just not now... She was getting deep-er into the lie.

"Wow...what are some of the kinds?" her father continued.

"Ah, well...the great white, hammerhead, tiger, mako... some other ones."

"Hey, don't forget the pretty good white, the half-decent white, the okay white, the I've-seen-better white... Then of course you have the wrench-head, the drill-head, the screwdriver-head..."

"Ha, ha, ha, Daddy. By the way, I already knew you were gonna say those jokes. I know your corny sense of humor by now."

"You're only saying that because it's true, you know."

"I know, Daddy. By the way, I knew you were gonna say that, too!"

"Well, since you always know what I'm going to say next, I guess it's not necessary for us to talk anymore!"

"Oh, Daddy... Please!"

"Hey, I've got a couple of cases that I want you to look at this weekend. There's a storeowner who thinks one of his employees is stealing. I want us to get some info…see if we can come up with a plan to catch him. Okay?"

"Sure, Daddy," Denise replied unenthusiastically.

When they got home Denise went straight to her room, changed, and did her homework. Her mother was working late, again, so she had dinner with her father and Jacob without exchanging more than a few words. Her mind was still going over a hundred things and rushing in so many different directions that she felt dizzy. She lay on her bed and thought about what her father told her when she was struggling with a decision. He always told her…figure out what's the right thing.

Denise thought it over. She had promised Domingo not to tell anyone, but that was before she knew so many people were being forced to work in that miserable place. This was *really* serious! She would also have to explain about going up to the mansion without any adults and lying about being at Mimi's house. That was against...well, let's see...EVERY RULE SHE WAS EVER GIVEN!

Aw, man, she thought. *What have I got myself into? But more importantly, what's the right thing? This mess has to be handled by grown-ups. I have to tell my father that I need help. Let's do this.*

As she slowly walked up to the door leading to the garage, Denise could hear the old rock and roll music and the clanking of metal. Her father was in the middle of one of his crazy CrossFit routines. Sure enough, when she opened the door, she saw him swinging a kettlebell—a round weight with a handle—up above his head over and over, grunting every time. He dropped the weight onto the black rubber mats on the floor. She knew better than to interrupt him—CrossFit was doing a couple of really intense things one after the other in cycles as fast as you can. It was incredible to watch, but it was usually over in twenty minutes. Denise glanced at the whiteboard her father had leaned against the wall.

"Helen"

3 rounds

400 meter run/ 30 kettlebell swings/ 12 pull-ups

You've gotta be kidding me! she thought.

Fortunately, he was on the last round. She saw him finish his pull-ups, jump down, and lie on the floor, his gray New England Patriots shirt dark with sweat. "Ooooh, ahhh, aaah- hhh! Hey, Niecey! Whooooo, whoooo!"

"Daddy, why do you do these workouts if they hurt so much?"

"Because it's hard, and it keeps me young!" her father gasped. "Your gymnastics workouts are hard...you can relate!"

"True. Hey, Daddy, I have to tell you something, but promise you won't get mad?"

The ex-captain felt a warm sensation in his stomach as a voice in the back of his head whispered a warning. *Something's up!* He turned serious, placed his face close to hers, and looked at her. She always got uneasy when he did that, because she knew he was "reading" her. He had trained her to watch someone's face when they were answering a question. After a while you could tell what they looked like when they were telling the truth and when they were lying. Her heart beat faster as she awaited his questions.

"I thought you'd been a little quiet, Niecey. C'mon, tell me what's going on."

Denise's mouth could not keep up with her brain, and the words came tumbling out of her, piling up until the incredible tale was revealed.

Like a good interviewer, Captain Lawson let his subject talk freely. He keyed on several phrases. Juarez...UPS truck...kidnap...mansion...contract...Grandpa...guard dog...Domingo...Taquito...hand sanitizer...boxes of chocolate... Jimmy the Pudding Boy...laundry baskets...dress factory...kids...

Finally she stopped. He could see that she was relieved to have passed this grown-up problem to the grown-up she trusted the most. He was proud, angry, and shocked all in the same moment.

"Niecey! I don't believe this! This is a criminal case with dangerous people! We have to go to the police, the FBI, Homeland Security, the Border Patrol… This is an international incident. What were you thinking?!"

Listening to her father, Denise could see that she and her friends had been playing a dangerous game. But she had given her word!

"Daddy," she sobbed, "I promised Domingo I wouldn't tell anyone because he was scared that something bad would happen to his mom and his grandpa!"

The ex-detective softened immediately and wrapped his arms around his brilliant and beautiful daughter. "I know, Niecey…I know. But you have to trust that the police and the federal agents are smart enough and experienced enough to go get these people *and* protect everyone at the same time. That's what they do. They're going to need our help, though, especially yours and your friends. I'm proud of you, little one, but we've got a lot of work to do!

"Tell me any details that you know are true. Do you have the exact address? What were the women and kids doing? How many people and guards are in the house? Did anyone see guns or weapons? What is Domingo's mother's name... the grandfather's name...the address in Mexico?"

He saw the panic on his daughter's face. "Niecey, I'm sorry. I'm overwhelming you. But this is a big deal and we have to act quickly. Let's start gathering all that information up. I'm going to call your uncle Frankie at the Border Patrol... He knows some guys in Homeland Security, and I think they have a task force for these kinds of cases...I hope they can get something together pretty quick."

Two hours later, Denise and her father were parking in front of a nondescript cement building not far from Denise's favorite shopping mall. Domingo was in the backseat, having just met Mr. Lawson in, shall we say, less than ideal circumstances. They got out of the SUV and started to walk toward the glass doors in front. Denise could see two uniformed officers at a big desk, through the glass. As they got closer another SUV pulled into a parking spot. She recognized the car as Mimi's grandfather's.

"Hey, Jack!" called Mr. Lawson. "What brings you out on such a beautiful night?"

"Couldn't sleep," the older gent replied slyly. "Thought I'd come out and re-live some of my youth." He and Mimi walked up to join the group.

By the strangest of coincidences, Mimi's grandfather, Jack DelaVega, was also a retired cop. In fact he had served as the chief of police in El Paso! The two men met because they both picked up the kids after school. They had hit it off because they loved talking about old cases. They liked to analyze crimes that were taking place in the news and brainstorm what they would do to solve them.

DANIEL LEYDON

"Did Mimi brief you?" Mr. Lawson asked seriously.

"Well, bare bones...they were lucky they got out of that place! I couldn't believe they would even try such a caper!"

"I know. But you have to give them credit for sticking up for someone who they thought was in trouble, even though they got in way over their heads."

"Someday, maybe I'll see it that way. Tonight, I'm mad. This is cutting into my beauty sleep."

Mr. Lawson laughed. "Yeah, you can use all you can get!"

Denise recognized Uncle Frankie in his green Border Patrol uniform when he opened the door for them. She glanced at Domingo. He was shaking like a leaf. Actually, Denise could now see why someone had made that phrase up...it described the situation perfectly.

"It's okay, Domingo," Mr. Lawson said softly. "These men only want to find your mother and shut down this horrendous operation. No one is going to lock you up."

The group was led up to a conference room, where they spent

the next few hours telling a team of agents what they had seen and heard. They were shown a blowup map of the mansion, and Denise pointed out the delivery entrance, elevator, and workshop. She handed over the dress label. Mimi and Domingo described the front of the house and the inside entrance. Spanish-speaking agents asked Domingo about his mother and grandfather.

It was almost midnight when a tall man with a white crew cut approached Captain Lawson and Jack. "We're still confirming some things, we've got eyes on the house, and our cross-border team is mobilized. Go home and get some rest and we'll let you know what the next step will be."

"Commander Garrity, that's a splendid idea!" Mr. Lawson replied. "These kids have had a day that they will never forget!"

With that the group shuffled toward the parking lot and headed home. Mr. and Mrs. Lawson had agreed that it would be best if Domingo stayed with them for the night. They had brought Taquito and Domingo's backpack to the house before going to the Federal Building.

As they pulled into his new friends' driveway, Domingo gaped silently at the spacious southwest home with its trimmed lawn. *This is a different world*, he thought. *I wonder if it will ever be my world?*

Mrs. Lawson had juice and sandwiches ready for them when they arrived. "You all should get right to bed," she ordered. "Tomorrow is Saturday, so you can sleep a little late. But Jacob has a soccer game at nine."

Denise hardly heard her. She was trying to make it look like it was every day that a handsome new crush stayed the night while an international law enforcement operation was unfolding. She thought she was doing a great job of it, too. She smiled reassuringly at Domingo. "What are you thinking?" she asked innocently.

"I am thinking about my mama," he whispered, holding back tears. "All she wanted was a chance to work and go to school. She wanted us to have a house and some nice things, like you. We did not see a way to get any of those things in my country. Now, she is trapped in a factory where she has to work so hard… I have no place to go, and my poor grandfather…" He couldn't finish. He looked down in silence, his face red. Denise saw a single tear slowly tracing a sad line down his face.

"I know, Domingo," Mr. Lawson said. "A lot of people see an opportunity here that they would not get anywhere else. They are willing to risk everything for a chance to work hard and improve their lives. Unfortunately, there are a lot of bad people who take advantage of people like you and your mother. It is a shameful crime, and that is why the penalties are so severe. These people will be caught, and they will pay for what they have done. Our country has laws against this sort of thing."

Mrs. Lawson quietly added, "You two were very brave in doing something about this. We are proud of you. Get some sleep. Hopefully you will be with your mother tomorrow, Domingo."

Denise fell fast asleep. She was right in the middle of one of her favorite dreams, where she was on stage at the spelling bee and just smoking! She was ready to spell "f-a-s-t-i-d-i-o-u-s" and move on to the final round when her dad came right up to the stage and began whispering loudly, "Niecey...Niecey!" She was totally annoyed.

Slowly it began to dawn on her that her cozy dream was over. Her father actually *was* waking her!

"The commander called me. The operation is going down; they want you to be there for afterward. We should go!"

Denise tried to understand the words she had just heard running through her brain. She was a notoriously bad morning person...really bad! She stared at her alarm clock in dismay. *It's 5:31? No way! I hate mornings!*

Suddenly she felt a surge of excitement. The operation was going down? She loved that kind of talk. It reminded her of when her father was in the police department and he would be part of so many big events. She used to love to try to see him on TV when the news came on.

Okay, then...for this I can be a morning person, she

decided, and pulled herself to a sitting position. "I'm up!" she crowed.

Remembering that her new friend would be joining her at breakfast, Denise looked over every hair bow in her collection and picked the perfect one for this occasion.

Domingo was already at the table gobbling down a Toaster Strudel. Denise joined him, but could not even taste the food. She was so excited it felt like she was floating above her body.

"Let's head out… Bring some water, my binoculars, flashlight, notepad, and pen…" Mr. Lawson was muttering to himself, going over his checklist of things to take on an "operation." Denise noticed that he shifted into a whole different person when things got serious, and it made her feel confident about what they were going to do.

As they drove toward the mansion, Mr. Lawson told them, "Listen, *we* are not going anywhere near this house. Commander Garrity wants you guys available to identify the people you saw, and of course, the main reason—to reunite Domingo with his mother! It might take awhile though, so be patient."

Mr. Lawson decided to drive to the kids' school. There was parking and shade, and it was about a mile from the mansion—or factory, or company, or whatever else this may end up being.

Mr. Lawson called Mimi's grandfather and filled him in. "Yeah, I figured I'd wait a little while to let you work on that elusive beauty sleep. Ha, ha! Yes, they may want Mimi to go up there later to show them where they went in and maybe to identify anyone they saw up there. What's that?" Mr. Lawson covered the phone. "Niecey, do you know anything about a bike and skateboards in Mimi's yard?"

Denise smiled to herself...the mad dash down the hill seemed like weeks ago, but it was only yesterday afternoon.

"They belong to a boy up the hill a little ways. We borrowed them, and we should bring them back."

Mr. Lawson drove over to Mimi's house, a few blocks away.

"Hey, Jack, hey, Mimi! Nice pajamas!"

Mimi's hair was tousled, eyes half shut, and she stood hunched over like a zombie…obviously asleep on her feet. But the pajamas were spectacular! Dozens of different breeds of dogs dotted every available inch of space. The buttons resembled little black pug noses with tiny breathing holes.

Denise and Domingo chuckled. "Those are adorable, Meems!" cried Denise. "You should wear those next Pajama Day at school."

"Yes, good thing we left Taquito in the car…he would be getting crazy jealous right now!" Domingo chimed in. The kids all laughed.

As the two ex-cops loaded Jimmy's stuff in the rear compartment, Jack asked, "Do you have a scanner?"

"Yeah, I haven't even turned it on yet, though," Mr. Lawson

answered. "Come on over later, when you're ready. I'm gonna drop these things off and then hang out at the school. It'll be like old times."

"Sounds good… I put the 'old' in old times!"

With everything loaded, the SUV began climbing toward Jimmy's house.

"I don't know the exact address, but I can show you where it is," Denise explained.

"Okay," Mr. Lawson said quietly as he switched on the police radio that he had attached to the inside of the glove compartment. He selected the right channel, adjusted the volume, and resumed driving.

Denise, Domingo, and Taquito were mesmerized by the staticky voice ticking off commands. "All units stand by. Perimeter positions, acknowledge when you are set up. Entry team, what is your ETA?"

"Aw, cool!" Denise exclaimed. "Where are they? What are they doing?"

Mr. Lawson patiently explained. "Well, they've set up a command post, and Commander Garrity is starting the operation. First, they set guys up in the back and side areas so no one will escape when the officers go to the house. They even have a helicopter nearby. Of course El Paso winds in January are really strong, so they have to be careful.

"The entry team will then try to get as close as they can without anyone seeing them. Then they'll have to get through the gates and into the house. Sometimes they have to knock doors down or disable gates…whatever it takes to get in quick and safe. The longer it takes, the more can go wrong." As he spoke he realized, once again, how badly he missed the excitement and camaraderie of his old occupation. He often wished that he was still doing it.

"Entry team, advise when you're in position. Air One, are you in the area?" the radio voice asked.

Denise and Domingo were staring at the radio, leaning forward in their seats. They couldn't believe this was happening...and at the same time they didn't really know *what* was going to happen. It was an anxious feeling that was difficult to control. They waited silently.

"Okay, move in! Move in!" they heard.

Then...silence...

"What's happening?" Domingo finally asked. Several seconds passed. No one breathed.

Mr. Lawson had been absentmindedly following the hill toward the top of the mountain. But the kids could see that he, too, was starting to worry about the situation. Denise recognized the street where Jimmy lived just up ahead. She was just about to say something when she felt a jolt that took her breath away.

"CODE 33! CODE 33! Subjects are fleeing in a black Humvee! One male dressed in all black...one female with white and yellow hair!" screamed a voice on the radio.

"What's the location?" Mr. Lawson recognized Commander Garrity's voice.

"They had an escape tunnel built into the garage! We can't follow because they shut a gate behind them. Two people got into a black Humvee and drove down the tunnel! Is the helicopter up?"

"Air One, what's your location?" the commander asked anxiously.

"We're circling, the winds are really bad. We can be there in a few minutes!"

"We don't have a few minutes!" the commander screamed. "Which way does that tunnel face?"

"It looks like it heads down the mountain, sir," reported a calmer voice, which Denise recognized as Uncle Frankie's.

Mr. Lawson had pulled over to the side of the road to concentrate on the radio talk. His heart was pumping adrenaline through his body, and he forced himself to take deep breaths to get control. He knew that the house was fairly close to where they were right now. He didn't want to get too close if the operation was still going on. It could be dangerous.

He was just about to turn and say something to Denise when, out of the corner of his eye, he thought he saw movement in a bush. The bush was about a half a block away on the same side of the street. As he watched, Mr. Lawson saw the bush roll onto the sidewalk. A tall man dressed all in black emerged from behind the bush. He quickly and methodically grabbed two more bushes and tossed them aside, revealing a narrow driveway and a hidden garage door. For a minute, Lawson thought that one of the police officers may be searching for the people from the house. His instinct told him that—no, this guy was one of the bad guys…he was trying to escape!

"Denise! Listen! I need you to do something!" Mr. Lawson barked.

Denise could tell something was wrong. By now she and Domingo had seen the man open the garage door and run inside.

"Denise…that's one of the guys. I need you to use my phone and call Commander Garrity. The number is in my contacts. I'm going to try and follow them if they start to move."

Before he had finished his sentence, a black Humvee inched out of the garage and onto the quiet street. Denise found the phone number and hit "Send."

"Captain, I'm a little busy. Can I call you back?" Commander Garrity growled curtly without saying hello.

"Commander, this is Denise Lawson! The black Humvee came out a secret driveway and we're chasing it! They're trying to get away!"

"Where are you?!" the commander howled.

By now the Humvee had picked up speed and was turning left down another street up ahead…they were going to lose sight of it! "Come on, Daddy! Step on it!" Denise implored. She barely could read the license plate. It read "C-M-P-N-Y."

Mr. Lawson gunned the engine and the big Sequoiasurged forward. Denise and Domingo felt like they were on a roller coaster freefalling down the big drop. At the corner Mr.

Lawson accelerated and muscled the steering wheel through the turn, causing them to lean all the way to the left amid the deafening sound of screeching tires.

"Get the street name," Mr. Lawson said loudly but steadily.

"Vista Lago Road," Denise dutifully replied. Although she was excited and her heart was pumping, she realized that it was important not to panic so they could get the cops back into the picture.

"Put the phone on speaker," her father ordered. Up ahead they saw the Humvee speeding down the street, fishtailing side to side. They could see the wheels of one side then the other almost coming off the ground.

"They know we're following them! Southbound Vista Lago Road! They're trying to lose us! The license plate is C-M-P-N-Y! Two aboard!" Mr. Lawson yelled into the phone. They could see the two people's faces in the rearview mirrors of the boxy black truck as it sped through two consecutive stop signs, barreling straight down the hill. Denise desperately tried to hold the phone steady and watch the wild scene in front of her.

"Commander, we need some assistance; they're heading south down Vista Lago, straight for the freeway! I've got two kids in the car. If they get to the freeway, they can make it to Mexico."

"We're on the way! Just give us a few minutes," the commander assured them.

They watched in horror as a young woman pushing a baby stroller with a pink balloon tied to the handle started walking into the crosswalk at the next stop sign.

"Nooooo!" they all shrieked in unison as Mr. Lawson leaned on the horn. "Look out!"

Miraculously, the woman looked up just in time to pull the stroller back a few feet. The Hummer roared by without slowing down at all. The woman with the stroller was kneeling down, crying and clutching her baby as they, too, roared by.

"They're gonna kill someone, Commander… I'm gonna have to stop them now! I'm gonna try a PIT maneuver!" Mr. Lawson declared.

A PIT is a police move where you stop a car by ramming it and making it spin out and stop. Under any circumstances, the captain knew it was risky, but these people were not stopping for anything, and there were several more crowded intersections ahead. Besides, if they got away, they probably would disappear forever and never be caught. This was his only chance.

The road started to level out as they descended the hill, and the street curved just a little to the right a few blocks ahead. The captain could see a small retaining wall on the left side, and immediately decided that this was where he would make his move. He saw the red brake lights of the Humvee as the driver slowed to anticipate the turn.

"You guys put your heads down and hold onto your knees. Whatever happens, don't get out of this truck! Understand?"

Denise and Domingo did as they were told. Denise closed her eyes, but in the blackness she heard her father's breathing, the engine racing, sirens in the distance, a heli-copter getting louder...and then WHUMP! Screeeeeccchhh! WHUMP!

The old detective drew on his experience, for he had done this maneuver successfully three or four times before. To do it right, it was crucial to match the speed of the oth-er car closely, make a little contact right behind their rear wheel, and accelerate till you feel them start to slide. Then you simply get off the gas and slow down. If all goes well, they spin once, you slow to a stop, and you are face-to-face with a stalled criminal.

And that's exactly what happened.

Denise heard the crunch and felt the car slow down and stop. She poked her head up to peer over her father's shoulder from the backseat. "Ha, ha! *It worked!*" The words exploded from her, she was so delighted.

She saw smoke coming from under the big truck's hood and could hear the grinding metal sound of someone trying to start a car. The big guy in all black was hunched over the steering wheel. He quickly looked up right at them, eyes wide open like a scared animal.

"He's going to run!" said Mr. Lawson. "You two wait here! Do not get out of the car... The cops should be right behind us. I'll take the driver! Keep your eyes on the woman! The cops will be here any second!"

He had barely finished speaking when the driver's door sprang open like a sideways jack-in-the-box. The driver had a big athletic build and moved gracefully onto the street. He turned and started sprinting down the hill; he leaped over the retaining wall like an Olympic hurdler and kept going. Denise could only watch his back as he got smaller and smaller. Her heart started to sink... He was getting away!

Then she caught sight of her father running down the street. He, too, jumped the wall like an Olympian, maybe a little older but, hey...he was moving *fast!* Maybe all his

CrossFit workouts had paid off! The two men disappeared from her sight within seconds.

The two friends were alone in the SUV. Suddenly Domingo gasped, "That's her!" pointing at the witch woman climbing out of the broken black truck.

"Who?" Denise turned to look.

"Her! That's the lady who bought me and my mother to work in her factory!" As he spoke they saw the wild-haired woman, wearing a leopard fur coat, pull a briefcase from inside the truck, walk to the retaining wall, and start hustling down the street. The police sirens sounded so far away!

Domingo choked back tears. "I can't let her get away! I'm going after her!"

Denise raised her voice for the first time to Domingo. "No! You heard my Dad...we wait for the police ... Just watch where she goes!"

The woman stopped, removed her fur coat, and tossed it

over the wall. She began to cover her head with a large scarf—
a beautiful red and gold scarf.

The sight was too much for Domingo. "My mother's
scarf! That's it!" He bolted from the car before Denise could
stop him. She followed as he sprinted full speed toward the
sidewalk.

The witch had tied the scarf tightly onto her head and
was now walking nonchalantly down the street with her
briefcase as if she didn't have a care in the world. Which she
didn't, unless you count a nine-year-old boy whose mother
had been kidnapped and grandfather menaced for the last
three days. Or a boy who had to sleep alone in an abandoned building without food, not knowing what was going
to become of him. So apparently she did have a care in the
world, and unbeknownst to her, it was zeroing in on her at
the maximum speed that this particular care in the world
could muster.

Denise looked over her shoulder and saw two police cars

with lights flashing pulling up to the two big cars sitting in the street. She turned back just in time to see the most beautiful tackle of a witch ever. Having grown up in San Francisco, the Forty Niners were her football team. She doubted that any of them could have done it any better. Of course they were not as motivated as her friend, Domingo. She saw two grown-up legs go from on the ground to about five feet in the air, as Domingo drove his shoulder into her ribcage, flipping her over the retaining wall perfectly and landing on top of her. The briefcase flew open and somersaulted through the air in a glorious slow-motion arc, papers flying everywhere in the gusty wind.

Domingo sat up and held the woman down with all his might.

"Aaarrrrgggghhh! What do you think you're doing, you cretin! I'll sue you for everything you have!" the woman screeched as Domingo kept her pinned like an MMA professional.

Suddenly she saw his face. *"You!"* she croaked.

"Yes, me!" Domingo declared triumphantly. "And you are in big trouble. Did you think you were going to be able to treat people like your personal slaves and no one was going to stop you?!"

"I've done it for years, you little creep, and no one's done anything about it yet."

"Yeah, well, that's because D&D Investigations wasn't on the case! You're gonna end up incarcerated. I-N-C-A-R-C-E-R-A-T-E-D!" Denise crowed as she walked up with four police officers in black SWAT gear. They were led by none other than her own uncle Frankie! "Arrest this lady, officers...she's a witch!"

"Wait one second, please." It was Domingo. Very deliberately, staring the evil one directly in the eyes, he reached up and snatched the scarf right off her head with a dramatic flourish. "This belongs to my mother! An ugly person like you does not deserve to wear anything so beautiful!"

Meanwhile, Mr. Lawson was running down his prey, trying to control his breathing and figure out what this guy was going to do. He already had noticed that the man was big and, judging by his shape, probably a weightlifter. Those guys usually get tired fast, but they're dangerous if they get hold of you.

Sure enough after about a minute, the big man slowed down. He looked up the hill over his shoulder and saw that his pursuer was catching up. He stopped suddenly to face the captain and make his stand. He bent down and picked up a big stick.

"Come on down, tough guy, I've got something for you!" he snarled menacingly.

The captain immediately thought of the *Terminator* movies...the thug was a dead ringer for Arnold Schwarzenegger. This was kind of funny!

Well, it was only funny because the old detective had noticed that this bad guy had made two really dumb mistakes in his tactics. Number one, he was downhill, so naturally, it was going to be easier to knock him over. Number two, he had stopped underneath a tree branch that stuck out a few feet above his head.

Mr. Lawson liked when things came together in a plan. These mistakes were going to make it simple for him to do *this*! He launched himself straight up, grabbing the tree branch with both hands like a trapeze artist. As he swung around the branch, he built up speed with his feet. He aimed for the wannabe movie star's solar plexus and scored a direct hit. The captain could hear and feel the air rush out of Arnold's lungs. The man tumbled backward, rolling two and a half times on the hill. He came to a stop in a heap, desperately fighting for air that wasn't coming. "Hhhooohhhh! Hhooooh! I can't breathe!" he finally managed.

"You'll be fine, tough guy. You could have killed someone driving like that. It serves you right."

The crumpled-up hoodlum was trying to come up with

an answer when three SWAT cops appeared from up the hill. "We'll take it from here, Captain. Get up, mister, you're under arrest!"

Seconds later, Denise, Domingo, and Taquito ran down to the spot, chattering excitedly. "Daddy, the witch lady tried to get away and Domingo tackled her. Uncle Frankie and his friends arrested her, and I think they found her briefcase!...Hey, that's the guy from the factory! Domingo, that's probably the same guy who chased you with the dog." She was on a roll and couldn't stop. "Hey, Arnold...not so tough now, are you! You should have known you wouldn't get away from D&D Investigations. My daddy does CrossFit... he could chase you all day. Oh, I guess you already know that by now, huh?"

The officers were holding the handcuffed hoodlum and searching him when Taquito squirmed out of Domingo's grasp and began barking his high-pitched yelps, leaping with all four paws off the ground on every yip.

Suddenly, he stopped, ran to the bad guy's feet, lifted his leg, and aimed a stream of water directly onto his shoes. At least it looked like water.

"He's peeing!" The kids laughed and pointed at the sight. Few things make kids laugh as much as unexpected bathroom activities, human or animal.

Mr. Lawson was grinning from ear to ear, but he turned serious. "Denise, I told you to stay in the car and wait! Why didn't you listen?"

Domingo spoke up. "Sir, that was my fault. I saw the lady wearing my mother's scarf and I decided that she had taken so much from us already. She took our money, our freedom, our family. But I saved all my money and gave my mother that scarf last Christmas. She cried happy tears when she opened it. I wanted her to have just one nice thing. This lady would not even let her have that; she had to take that away, too. I told myself, no. She is not taking the thing that ties me to my mother in spirit. I forgot that I was nine years old, I forgot that I was in America, and I forgot what you told me about staying in the car. I only knew that I could see the one thing that represented my family disappearing, and I was not going to let that happen. I told myself that I would do anything--*anything*--to get that scarf back. Once my mind was made up, my body took over and the rest was easy."

"I can understand, Domingo," Mr. Lawson said quietly. "Your mother and grandfather should be proud."

Denise fought back tears and gave Domingo a quick hug. "Man, that lady went *down,* baby!" The two kids exchanged high fives as everyone headed back up to the street.

A tow truck was backing up to the Humvee, and what seemed like every police officer and state and federal agent in El Paso swarmed the road. Denise could see Commander Garrity standing right in the middle, pointing fingers and talking into a walkie-talkie. The helicopter went whump - whump - whump - whump over the smoking mansion.

Denise could hear the mean woman cackling from the

backseat of a police car as she squirmed, her vile mouth spewing ugliness. "You've got nothing on me. You won't find one record or shred of evidence in that house. I made sure of that. And maybe you didn't notice the papers from the briefcase flying all over this mountain! I'm just a small businesswoman trying to make a living!"

Denise got a bad feeling when she heard that and started contemplating if maybe the woman was right. She looked down the street and saw dozens of papers sailing in the wind like balloons that had slipped from a little kid's grasp. Maybe she *was* smart enough to destroy all the evidence.

Her thoughts were interrupted by the arrival of a nondescript blue SUV with black tinted windows slowly inching through the sea of uniforms. The rear door swung open and Denise could see a streak of white.

Domingo's mom, brown hair streaming behind her, raced onto the street still wearing a white work smock. "Domingo! Domingo?!"

"Here, Mama! I am here!" Denise felt her new friend rush by her and into his mother's open arms.

"Oh, my son, my son! I knew you would find me! I love you, hijo, I love you more than anything!" she cried. Her eyes were closed as she savored the feel of her only child rocking back and forth in her arms.

"*Y Papa?*" Domingo croaked.

"He is safe, son. They found him and he is fine, thanks to you and your friends. The *policia* told me about what you did!"

Tears streamed down Denise's face as she stared at the emotional reunion.

"Remember this feeling, Niecey. It doesn't come very often in our kind of work, but when it does it makes all the hard work and frustration worth it."

Denise moved close and wrapped her arm around her special business partner.

A distinctive accent broke their moment. "Hey, take it easy, fellas. This is only temporary. My lawyer is going to have me out before you guys even write the report!" The thug

chuckled. "Hey, look! It's snowing paper! Unusual weather

for El Paso, huh?! Ha, ha, ha!"

Sure enough, it was the handcuffed Terminator being his

usual blowhard self while being led into the big black-and-

white police wagon.

As Denise watched, she saw Domingo's mother's eyes

turn into narrow slits, and her mouth became a snarling twist

of teeth and spit. "You!" She stood up and took a step toward

the wagon. The air filled with Spanish words that Denise had

never heard before as the petite woman launched herself at the

black-clad creep.

Mr. Lawson stepped in just in time to prevent another knock-

down of everyone's favorite European evildoer. Commander

Garrity also hurried over to make sure the situation didn't get

out of hand.

"You horrid monster! How could you treat people like

that?" Carmella exclaimed. "Working us fourteen hours a day?

One break for food…unbearable heat…no days off? You and her are monsters and now the whole world is going to know!"

"Yeah, yeah! Guess again. The computers and records have been destroyed. Our lawyers have valid contracts from Mexico! You've got nothing!"

"Oh no! The computers have been destroyed?…the records burned?…the lawyers have contracts? What are we going to do?" Domingo's mother wailed.

"Yeah…too bad, huh?" the witch screeched from the police car.

Carmella turned to look at the woman who up until twenty minutes ago was her boss.

"Now you're getting it!" Schwarzenegger sneered at her. "Might as well take the cuffs off me now, officers!" He started to turn away from his accuser.

"Hey…wait a minute," Carmella said slyly. She lifted up her foot and removed her tennis shoe. "What in the world is this?" She removed the sole and brought out a small black rectangle, which she dramatically held between her thumb and forefinger about six inches from his face.

"You don't suppose a stupid, ignorant factory worker without a college education could figure out how to copy files onto a thumb drive, do you? Nooo, she is only good for sewing dresses seven days a week… She probably didn't even notice that we were putting designer labels onto your cheap clothes and charging stores for the real thing. And she's definitely waaay too stupid to make copies of the real tax returns of The Company for the last five years…because she is not from here and does not speak too good English! Well, how's this for good English, you soon-to-be federal prisoners—hasta la vista, *BABY! I QUIT!*"

Every officer on the scene had dropped what they were doing to listen to this little package of dynamite deliver her spontaneous resignation speech. There were a few seconds of silence and then…wild applause and cheers arose from the crowd of lawmen as the terrible twosome was driven away. Everyone loved to root for the underdog.

Commander Garrity was chuckling and shaking his head admiringly. "Lady, this is one for the books. I thought they had escaped our trap and covered their tracks. Between D&D Investigations and you and your kid, we're back in business. Let's go, men, we still have a lot of work to do. Captain, be at the Federal Building with our guests of honor in about an hour."

"Mrs. Ventana, you can come with us now," Mr. Lawson said gently. "I know you've been through a lot, but you'll have to talk to the investigators. Commander Garrity told me that the State Department will be sending someone to see about keeping you and Domingo here for a while." He looked over her shoulder and could see that Domingo was waiting to say something to his mother. He turned away to give them privacy.

"Mama…" Domingo called.

She turned to face him. He was standing with his head bowed and his hands behind his back. She saw a teardrop flash and land on the ground, making a starburst on the dusty El Paso pavement.

"What is it, mijo?" she replied lovingly.

"Merry Christmas," he sobbed as he handed her the red and gold scarf that had almost disappeared from his life forever.

"Oh, mijo! Thank you! I could never ask for anything better!" She squeezed him tightly, unable to say anything else.

Denise was enjoying the turn of so many emotional events but suddenly remembered something.

"Oh, oh! Where's Taquito?" she asked in a panic. "Taquito! Taquito! Oh no!"

Mr. Lawson stood on the floorboards of the Sequoia and scanned the scene. After a couple of sweeps, a big smile began to spread across his face. "Denise, who is every dog's best friend?"

"Ah, I don't know...man?"

"Who also happens to be your best friend?"

"Mimi!" Denise sang out. "Do you see her?"

"She and Jack are waving to me. They're walking over now."

"Hey, I heard you guys had to save the day...was it Batman's day off or what?" Jack yelled, a giant grin beaming across his face.

"Ha, ha. Yeah, D&D Investigations rides again. The Ventanas here look like they could give us a run for our money if they put their minds to it, though!"

Mimi trotted over with Taquito firmly in her grasp. "Is it true that Domingo tackled the witch lady?"

"Aw, Meems, *it was epic!* You should have seen it. Then my dad took down Arnold Schwarzenegger! It was the best day ever!"

"Well, it's even better than you thought," Jack chimed in. "According to Commander Garrity, they set up a sting over in Juarez. They caught the couple that set up the phony contract and the job placement scam. Then they got the UPS guy when he showed up with his rigged-up truck. Homeland Security is really happy; they've been hearing about this group, but they couldn't figure out what they were doing or how they were doing it."

"That's because they didn't have D&D Investigations on the case!" Mr. Lawson said with a laugh.

Slowly, he, Jack, and Mrs. Ventana turned and looked at the three nine-year-olds. They were taking turns having Taquito lick their faces and laughing hysterically. They didn't have a care in the world.

"You know, I wish there was a way to bottle what those kids have right now, and keep it for them till they get older," Mr. Lawson said. "It's really fleeting, and these things don't always have a happy ending."

"Boy, are you corny!" Jack said with a roll of his eyes.

"Too much?" Mr. Lawson asked, grinning.

"Not really...I'm just teasing. I understand what you're saying."

"C'mon, kids, get in the car; we should get going," the ex-detective called.

Denise and Domingo piled in the back with Taquito. Mrs. Ventana sat in the passenger seat.

As they slowly weaved through the officers and the crime technicians, they could see a large group gathered just outside the yellow police tape. Denise recognized the woman from the news show about the flu epidemic, holding a microphone with the letters K-P-E-P. A man with a news camera was standing behind her. Several other teams were setting up their equipment while more news vans were still trying to park.

"Holy smokes!" Denise exclaimed. "I've never seen so many news people in my life, have you?"

"Oh, yeah," her dad replied with a little sigh. "This brings-back memories for me. Luckily, the good guys won today, so the press is our friend!"

"Captain Lawson! Captain Lawson!" The reporter waved. "Can we have a word with you?"

"Sure, just for a minute, though," Mr. Lawson answered. "We've got to get going."

"Great, thanks! This is Vivian Vachon, KPEP News, live with the private detectives who broke open this highly shocking case of kidnapping and human slavery. We understand that the operation extended from the barrios of Juarez to right here in one of the most exclusive neighborhoods of El Paso. Former San Francisco Police Captain Dennis Lawson, head of D&D Investigations. How did you crack this case?"

Dennis Lawson casually leaned out the driver's side window and replied, "Actually, my partner did the majority of the work. She figured out that there were people being held in an illegal clothing factory up here in the hills. She got the exact location, found evidence of what was going on, and brought it to the police. You can see the result when the police tried to move in."

"That is very impressive. Who is this partner and can we speak with them?"

"Oh, sure. Hey, Niecey! Come on up here!"

Denise didn't have to be asked twice, for despite what she

sometimes said, she was not very shy when it came to cameras. She hastily put on some peppermint lip gloss, climbed up front, and knelt on the console next to her father. The cameraman zoomed in on her face. She looked in the rearview mirror and straightened her lucky sparkly red hair bow.

"This is my partner," the detective said, "and she's also my daughter. D and D stands for Denise and Daddy. I'm Daddy."

As he spoke, he could see the other camera crews pointing their lenses at them. He felt a little uneasy, but he wanted Denise to have a moment of recognition, too.

"Do you mean to tell me that a ten-year-old girl solved this case? It's an international smuggling and counterfeit trademark operation!"

"No, no, no...don't be silly. A ten-year-old could never do that," Mr. Lawson acknowledged, pausing for dramatic effect. "She's *nine* years old!"

"Young lady, this is incredible! What made you such a good crime fighter?"

"Well," Denise smiled, "you have to trust your instincts, have a plan, and always do the right thing! That's what my father taught me, and that's what my friends and I did!"

"Thank you, miss. And that's the story from Red Mountain, where two people are under arrest and an illegal operation has been shut down, thanks to the brilliant detective work of a nine-year-old girl! This is Vivian Vachon, KPEP News."

As they began to inch forward, Denise recognized the familiar round shape of an old friend.

"Hey, Denise! I knew you guys were up to something when you were up here. But I had no idea it was something as cool as this. Wow!" shouted Jimmy the Pudding Boy as he rode alongside the car.

"Yeah, well, it was kind of a secret mission, Jimmy. No hard feelings, huh? Oh, hey, we've got your bike in the back."

"You're kidding right?" Mr. Lawson asked in disbelief. "*That's* the kid whose bike you have?"

"Yeah, he lives up here!"

"Is he your age? He's so... *big!*"

"That's Jimmy the Pudding Boy, Daddy. I'll tell you about him later."

They pulled ahead to the curb and gave Jimmy his bike. He started laughing hysterically and pedaling around like a rolling mound of putty with a hat.

"What's so funny, Jimmy?" Denise asked.

"I was thinking about seeing that evil lady flying upside down without a broom, like most witches!"

"Wait a minute! You *saw* that?" Denise was shocked.

"Saw it? I did better than that. You underestimate me! But you'll see!"

"Everybody does that, Jimmy!" chimed in a small but sturdy voice.

And who suddenly appeared attached to this little voice?

"No way! Brutus!" Denise roared with laughter. "What are you doing here? This crime wave is attracting the most intriguing audience!"

The little terror smiled and said, "Jimmy's my cousin, Denise. Hey, is it true you and your dad captured the evil witch that lives in that creepy mansion?"

Denise laughed. "Is that what you heard, Brutus? No. We helped but there were a whole lot of people working on this. There were some really bad people running a nasty business right here in your neighborhood!"

"I believe you! Me and Jimmy were always scared of that place. They had mean dogs and guards! And we saw that lady! Ugh!"

The excitement over for now, the group made its way back to what was sure to be a more mundane portion of the whole operation—the paperwork.

Chapter Six

The Lawsons waited in the parking lot of the Federal Building for Mimi and her grandfather, and walked back up to the offices of the Task Force. Domingo and his mother were chattering away in an avalanche of Spanish and weeping with a heavy dose of full-force hugging. Their joy was contagious. While they were apart, they had been afraid but determined. Together they were confident and more formidable than ever. Domingo felt so proud to be his mother's son.

"Señora Ventana?"

"Si, señor." Mrs. Ventana looked up to see a tall Hispanic man about her age holding the door to an interview room open. Carmella felt a sudden rush of heat run through her body. Something about this man seemed familiar.

Carmella entered the room and seated herself at a small table. The tall man and two others introduced themselves as

Task Force members. They began taking her statement and showed her photographs for her to identify. The couple from Juarez, the UPS driver, the awful yellow-haired witch, and, of course, Arnold Schwarzenegger.

They took the thumb drive, a notebook, and a handful of phony "designer" tags that Carmella had gathered as evidence. They asked her questions for a long time, until finally, the story was out and everyone relaxed.

Commander Garrity entered the room. "Ma'am, you and your boy have shown a great deal of courage and spirit. Those are things that we value here in America. You have helped us stop these people from taking advantage of innocent women and children who wanted nothing more than a chance at a better life. We are in your debt."

The tall man stood and shyly spoke. "Carmella, do you remember me?"

Carmella stared and a quick memory flashed through her mind like the flit of a butterfly. She saw a young boy in scruffy clothes standing on the seat of an old bicycle as it wobbled down the only hill in the neighborhood. She saw herself rush to help the boy when he fell over the handlebars. She saw herself holding him until he began to smile.

"Marco, is it you? I thought I knew you! It's been so long!" Carmella gushed in amazement. She was staring at a grown-up professional investigator but seeing a little boy she played alongside of as a carefree little girl. She felt the innocence of that time return, and it felt so good.

"Yes. I work for the Mexican authorities now. My father and I still live in Juarez. He manages several factories over there."

The two began chatting as if thirty years and a million pieces of life had not even occurred. They were just two neighborhood kids who wanted to live their dreams.

Mimi, Domingo, and Denise had met with the detectives and told their stories. They all felt a little thrill when they were asked to look at the photographs of the evil witch and her associates. They didn't look so big and scary in the pictures for some reason.

Captain Lawson and his friend Jack had been with Uncle Frankie and his friends writing reports and answering questions.

It took a few hours but finally it was all over. Commander Garrity gathered everyone into a conference room and said, "It's been a long day; it's almost five o'clock. Thank you all for your hard work and perseverance today. Every now and then you get to go home feeling good, like you made a difference out there. Today's one of those days. Congratulations.

"There's one more thing... I'm not exactly sure what's going on, but this thing is really taking off in the media. Our public relations people are getting swamped with interview requests. Let's go out, answer a few questions, and we'll be done."

Puzzled, the Lawsons and Ventanas exchanged glances,

but did as they were told. They followed the commander, Uncle Frankie, and a few others through a door and right on to a low stage. Two long tables with microphones stood near the front. Bright lights from above glared down at them, and dozens of teams of reporters, some with cameras, some without, jammed several rows of seats.

"Aw, man!" exclaimed Mr. Lawson. Memories of hiscrime-fighting days were mostly positive, but he had always cringed at the press conferences. He preferred to let his work speak for itself. But he knew that his precocious daughter would be thrilled. He glanced at her and could see breathless wonder and excitement coming out of her like the glow of an evening star.

The handsome commander strode to a podium on the stage as the others took seats at the long tables. "Good afternoon, folks, I'm Commander Garrity of the El Paso Major Crimes Task Force. Today, we successfully shut down a kidnapping and human trafficking ring. We made several arrests and located an illegal garment factory that was producing counterfeit designer clothing. So to say this was a successful operation is an understatement. To my team, congratulations on a job well done! Of course, it didn't go exactly the way we planned, but these things never do. Thank goodness for the backup team, ex-San Francisco Police Captain Denny Lawson and his daughter Denise, better known as D&D Investigations, and of course the victims who refused to be victims, Carmella Ventana and her son Domingo."

As the commander spoke, he pointed out the reluctant heroes, although it seemed that everyone already knew who they were.

No sooner did he finish when a pretty blond reporter holding a microphone with the red letters C-N-N yelled out, "Have you seen the video?"

For the first time, Denise saw the commander a little flummoxed. She loved that word but didn't like seeing the poor commander living it.

Suddenly all eyes were on a big-screen TV set up on the stage. A YouTube video was loaded up. The graphic had one word: "Payback!" Someone clicked the "Play" arrow.

Up on the screen, Denise recognized the family Sequoia from the soccer decal on the back. The driver's door was flung open and the car was stopped at a sharp angle. On the sidewalk ahead, the whitehaired witch-lady was tying the scarf around her hair and carrying her briefcase. Like a lightning bolt, Denise saw Domingo explode from the rear door...seeming to open the door, sprint down the street, and smash through his nemesis in a split second. She heard a loud "Oooohhhh!" from the crowd as a missile called Domingo blasted into his target. The woman's head disappeared over the wall and her feet sawed away at the air. A boy's laughter was barely audible as Denise Lawson jumped out of the vehicle and joined the action, arriving as Domingo was reclaiming his cherished scarf from the defeated woman. Uncle Frankie appeared and led her away.

"Now, that is what I call a tackle!" exclaimed the distinctive voice that she now recognized as none other than Jimmy the Pudding Boy. And then the video ended.

So that's what he was talking about! she thought

Cameramen jostled for position near the front of the stage as what seemed like a hundred people asking a thousand questions rose to a deafening crescendo.

Denise could feel her cheeks warming up. She knew she was blushing, which she considered one of her least flattering looks.

Oh no, she thought. *Everything is happening so fast. The one time in my life that everyone is going to be looking at me and I'm gonna look just like a dork!*

But then she felt something soft and strong grip her hand. She looked under the table and saw a brown hand wrapped around hers. Domingo! He looked at her, winked quickly, and nodded his head as if to say, "It's all good, you got this!" After what they'd been through the last few days, she realized that this was true. Confidence and pride showed on her face, and she felt like she could do anything!

In what seemed like a one-hour dream, Denise and Domingo, the captain and Carmella, and even occasionally Commander Garrity and Uncle Frankie answered questions about human smuggling, UPS trucks, evil witches, scary henchmen, and a factory for phony designer clothes. The press loved it!

But the press fell in love with Denise more than anyone. The questions came like the gush of a waterfall, and her answers bounced back without hesitation.

Yes, she liked working with her daddy.

No, he wasn't jealous because their company wasn't DADDY and Denise. ("He knows I'm the brains of the outfit," she declared.)

Yes, this was her lucky hair bow. Yes, she collected them.

Yes, that was her in the spelling bee last month.

When she grew up, she was going to be an author....

Over the years, Dennis Lawson had seen so many despicable and evil people that he had long ago lost count. He took the capture of these people so seriously, he worked around the clock on many occasions. He had come to understand that total dedication by good detectives was sometimes the only thing stopping bad people from hurting innocent victims. He was always willing and happy to pay that price.

As he glanced at his incredible, blossoming daughter confidently bantering with the national press, he saw another positive force developing right before his eyes. He swelled with pride and stifled a sob.

His main concern during his aging years was guessing what kind of a world his children would inherit. He was starting to see that, no matter what world came to be, this beautiful young lady was going to be actively involved in shaping it. She would not only survive; she would thrive.

Downstairs, the Lawsons noticed the Ventanas in a serious conversation with a man and woman dressed in almost identical suits. *That's odd*, Denise thought, since one was a woman. She remembered that her mother dressed in suits for work sometimes, but it looked weird with a man and woman wearing the same thing. *Just sayin!* she thought, but didn't say.

The Ventanas signed some papers and excused themselves. They joined Carmella's tall neighborhood friend in a small side office and after a few minutes, all walked out together.

The Lawsons had been making small talk with Mimi and her grandfather. Everyone was more than ready to call it a day.

"What did they tell you? Can you stay in the United States?" Mr. Lawson asked eagerly.

"We qualify for special circumstances they say, but we declined their offer," Carmella replied. Lawson could detect pride in her tone. "My friend Marco has arranged for me to work for his father. He owns some businesses in Juarez, and is in need of a bookkeeper. He has a program that helps employees go to college, and I am going to enroll in a business school that I know about. With a degree, perhaps I can start my own business someday." Carmella's eyes flared with excitement as she spoke.

"I don't understand. I thought you were looking for a new life here."

"No, my new friend. I am simply looking for an *opportunity* where I am allowed to work and to be treated fairly. I now see that I can do that in my country. I love my country, I love my city, and I love my family!" Carmella continued.

"I know that," Mr. Lawson told her.

"I intend to study, work hard, and succeed! I expect my son to study, work hard, and succeed! My father is old and confused about how his home has been slowly turned into a place of despair and hopelessness, where everyone leaves to find a better life. To run would only add to that despair. Someone has to stay and fight back!" She was getting emotional as she poured out her thoughts.

"Wow, Carmella." The ex-detective was impressed.

"Dennis, you and your daughter have taught us a valuable lesson. Age and size are not important in accomplishing things. Your heart, your determination matter. There is no guarantee that we will succeed, but we know that we can and we know that we will. Good-bye, sir, and thank you for your kindness."

She reached up and hugged him, and he could see her struggling to keep from crying. He felt himself doing the same.

Mimi and Domingo were finishing a quiet conversation when Carmella called, "Domingo, say thank you and good-bye to your friends. We have much more to do. Marco is going to bring us to Papa now."

Domingo felt like his stomach was in a washing machine. All the soaring emotions that came with victory, revenge, and reunion suddenly crashed to earth. In their place came a terrifying fear that he would never again see the people who stood with him during the craziest days of his life. A time filled with such a relentless seesaw of extremes wasn't supposed to end so abruptly, like a youth soccer game!

One look at Denise's face told him that she was feeling the

same way. Her eyes looked at him pleadingly, her mouth open...
but no magical words of inspiration would come this time.

"We showed them that kids can take care of business,
didn't we, amigo!" she managed with a shy smile.

"We sure did, amiga. You were awesome. Maybe we can
come visit sometime. I can read your books and you can read
my poetry!" Domingo replied bravely, unable to look his angel
in the eye.

"Yeah!" Denise choked, almost sobbing.

Mercifully the adults began walking to the door with their
car keys in hand...the universal sign for *exit*.

Mr. Lawson brought Domingo's backpack over to the gov-
ernment car in which Marco was driving the Ventanas. As he
passed it, Domingo gave him a quick glance and shush gesture
that wordlessly entered them into an agreement. He placed a
folded square of paper into the old detective's hand and stared
straight ahead. Shimmering wet streaks trickled from his eyes
to his chin.

Denise silently watched first Marco's and then Mimi's cars ease out of the yard so effortlessly that it was hard to believe such a feeling of emptiness could result. Her cheeks were on fire and she felt like something was blocking her throat.

It was dark when they gently rolled into their driveway and walked into the house.

"There are about ten messages from all over the place!" Stella Lawson began breathlessly. "Security reps from Justice and Aeropostale want to know if you're available to investigate counterfeit clothing cases. One of your ex-police chiefs called to razz you. Newspaper people, TV people...you name it! I cannot believe what a big deal this is, especially after that viral video came out!"

"Yeah...we are the flavor of the day, I think." The captain chuckled, squeezing his wife and lifting her into the air. "I can't wait till Jacob is able to join us on the team!"

Suddenly they noticed Denise slumped on the couch with her head in her hands. You'd never know that a few hours ago, she was on top of the world.

"Hey, Niecey."

Denise looked at her father through her hands.

"Someone wanted me to give you this." He handed her the folded paper.

Denise took it and began to read. Mr. Lawson began reviewing the phone messages with his wife and taking notes.

A deep sob arose from the couch, and they turned to see the back of their precious daughter as she ran up the stairs.

Mrs. Lawson went to the couch and read the paper that Denise had left behind, slowly lifting her hand to her mouth. "Oh boy!" she whispered softly.

The captain saw two hand-drawn red hearts at the top of the page and read:

Someone, Somewhere
When my sunny world vanished, I was forced to hide.
All alone, miles from home, with no one at my side.
I prayed, Let there be Someone, Somewhere

to help me turn the tide.
And then a burst of light appeared—a CHILD?—
this can't be real.
It was YOU—my Someone, Somewhere!
And my world began to heal.
The power and the confidence I saw
flashing through your eyes
Told me this Someone, Somewhere
could lift me and we'd rise.

Rise we did with power that was far beyond our years.
You guided us and taught us
that we all could squash our fears.
Somehow we forced ourselves
to where we'd never dared before.
With Someone, Somewhere leading us,
we found power, but much more.

Then somehow we succeeded—
the trapped one now on top,
All those helpless feelings came screeching to a stop.
Though I go now to the open air, my family, my new start
I'll keep my Someone, Somewhere forever in my heart.

Denise,

Thank you for changing my life!

Tu amigo,

Domingo

"I suggest we just let her be for a while. I don't care how mature she is for her age. This is a whirlwind that anyone of any age would be struggling to deal with!" Stella proclaimed.

Eventually, after they had given Denise plenty of time to cry, or whatever she needed to do to figure out how to feel, they walked into her room together. Dennis quietly placed the poem on her nightstand. Denise followed the paper with her eyes. Her head didn't move.

"You know, little one, it was a brave decision that Carmella and Domingo made today. They chose to stay and work in their own country, even though it will be harder. They believe it is more important to be part of the generation that changes and improves things. I admire both of them for their loyalty."

"I know, Daddy. It's just that everything happened so fast, I barely got a chance to really get to know them."

Stella spoke up. "Denise, it might help to write your thoughts down in your journal. Or maybe write a story about this adventure. You're such a good writer!"

"Yeah, I have every intention of writing this story. I also can't wait to see the faces of my classmates on Monday, especially my arch-nemesis! This is gonna be awesome!" Denise crowed.

"True, but don't forget the real reason that we do this, and it isn't to make other kids know how cool you are," Mr. Lawson scolded good-naturedly. "Besides, judging by our phone messages, we're going to be busier than ever. I hope you're ready for this!"

"Oh, I was born ready, Daddy!"

"Yes, you were. I remember well!" Mrs. Lawson exclaimed with a hearty laugh.

Chapter Seven

Monday morning rose bright and early, and as usual, Dennis Lawson had to beg, order, threaten, plead, and bargain his two kids out of bed, down to breakfast, into their clothes, and finally, off on their way. Denise and Jacob's standard bickering session was background noise for him.

"Some things never change," he muttered to himself. Rolling down Interstate Ten he passed Sun Bowl Stadium, home of the University of Texas at El Paso Miners on his left. Everyone in El Paso used I-Ten on a regular basis.

He looked out the passenger window on his right. Just a few hundred yards away, he could see Mexico waking up, probably at the same pace. That casual glance toward the jumble of beat-up wooden homes, mostly brown, the bare cocoa-colored mountains, even the bustling cars and trucks in the busy streets represented something much more meaningful and personal to him now. There was a story over there that would forever be a part of him, he thought. Somehow he was confident, those same feelings would steal their way into his daughter's thoughts very soon.

Arriving at school, Mr. Lawson was shocked by the scene playing out as they turned into the parking lot. "Is Shakira giving a show today, or what?"

"What are you talking about?" Denise asked...just as she noticed exactly what her father was talking about.

A huge throng of kids surrounded Denise and Mimi's favorite picnic table, the one where they met every morning. She could barely see the top of her best friend's head as the other kids swarmed like ants on an old peppermint. Her grandfather hovered nearby, looking perplexed. Denise silently spelled p-e-r-p-l-e-x-e-d. Yep, she felt mostly like she always did, but she couldn't help but feel in her gut, her *instinct,* that *something* was different.

"I guess there's a new star of the show!" Mr. Lawson chuckled. "Wait till you get out there!" As they unloaded, he added cautiously, "Don't get overwhelmed, little one. You're still the same person."

"Yeah," Jacob chimed in, "a pain in the…"

"Oh, be quiet, you little pest!" Denise snapped.

"All right, you two, that's enough. I'll be close by, Niecey."

The captain wandered off to have his usual morning meeting with his friend Jack, while his kids were quickly swallowed up by a sea of curiosity and awe. They'd have a little more than the usual chitchat to catch up on today, though!

Kids and parents from every grade in school were firing questions and telling stories about the big adventure that made El Paso a national news story.

"I saw you on the TV. That hair bow looked so cool!"

"Did you see Jimmy's video? That was awesome!"

On and on it went as Denise, Mimi, and even Jimmy were the center of attention for a good twenty minutes. Of course this day was no different than any other, and the bell soon rang, signaling the students to line up.

As Denise slowly walked toward the fourth-grade line, she heard a familiar cringe-inducing voice.

"I suppose you think you're something special all of a sudden, huh? Well, forget it. Your hair still looks like rats live in there—and can you give me a break with those stupid hair bows? You're not four years old, you know!"

Mandy!

Denise instinctively hunched her shoulders and hung her head. Her stomach flip-flopped and she felt like she couldn't breathe, let alone talk. *I guess some things never change after all,* she thought, ashamed.

Out of the corner of her eye, Denise suddenly caught a glimpse of a fifth-grade girl making her way to class. The girl was tall and thin and was wearing a red and gold scarf around her head. Denise immediately thought of Carmela Ventana. She smiled to herself, felt a warm glow, and in that very second, she knew everything was going to be okay.

She marched straight up to her archenemy and stood

squarely in front of her—toes almost touching toes. She drew herself up as tall as she could, knowing that she was bigger than her foe. She put her nose about three inches from Mandy's and glared directly into her eyes.

"You know what, Mandy? I don't care what you say, what you feel, or what you think of me. You are so insignificant to me that you may as well not even exist. But, do you know something? I'm bigger than that... I actually feel sorry for you. The only way you can make yourself feel good is by making other people feel small and powerless. But guess what? That doesn't make you better... It makes you mean. It makes you a bully! And no one likes a bully! So, go ahead and make your little comments. If I cared even one iota about what you thought of me, they might bother me. But I don't. So they don't! And do you know what today is, Mandy? It's my Independence Day! From this day on, I am *never, ever* going to let your comments get to me again! Am I making myself clear, Mandy, or can't you understand someone who smells like rotten eggs. Get a life! And leave me alone!"

Mandy stood with her mouth open for a second. Then she covered her mouth with her hand for two seconds, and tears silently began to run down her cheeks. She ran to the classroom. Niecey followed, head high and shoulders straight.

As the rest of the class settled in, Denise looked over at her BFF. Mimi locked eyes with her, silently nodded her head, and held out her fist. Denise smiled, a little embarrassed, and wordlessly fist-bumped her friend. The friends showed once again that even without saying anything, they could communicate better than anyone anywhere. Of course she was the "Someone, Somewhere," so that only made sense.

Two older-looking gentlemen slowly sauntered to their family trucks. They had more than sixty-five years of experience fighting crime between them. Nevertheless, they looked at each other with the same question in their eyes.

"Have you ever seen anything like this in your life?" ex-captain Dennis Lawson asked ex-chief Jack DelaVega.

"Nope, never. But unless I miss my guess, with those two girls and your boy coming up, I think things are going to get a whole lot crazier before they get duller! And you know what? I don't think you'd want it any other way!"

As he climbed into the front seat, Dennis Lawson said loudly "You got that right, partner. As they say on the ranch, hang on to your hats!"

The End

CPSIA information can be obtained
at www.ICGtesting.com
Printed in the USA
FSOW01n0517110915
10964FS

9 781478 745976